HOME FOR CHRISTMAS IN JULY

A MISTLETOE MOUNTAIN NOVEL

MELISSA F. MILLER

BROWN STREET BOOKS

PLAYLIST

Here's a collection of songs to listen to while you read *Home for Christmas in July*. Add a cozy corner and your favorite beverage and you'll be all set. You can also find the playlist on my website, www.melissafmiller.com.

"Please Come Home for Christmas," Vonda Shepard
"River," Robert Downey, Jr.
"Love Don't Die Easy," Charlie Worsham
"Hiding Place," Miranda Frigon
"Come Home to Me," American Authors
"I'll Take You," Miranda Frigon
"This Love (Taylor's Version)," Taylor Swift
"I'll Be Home for Christmas," Sara Evans
"All I Want for Christmas Is You," Michael Bublé
"Second Chance," Cast of High School Musical: The Musical
"Rainbows," Kacey Musgraves
"Here Comes the Sun," Yo-Yo Ma, James Taylor

"A Thousand Years," Christina Perri

"Dreamers," Oh Gravity

"I'll Be Home for Christmas," Jimmy Buffett (yes, this song again)

"Wide Awake," Aimée Proal

"The Way We Never Say Goodbye," Travis James

"You Make It Feel Like Christmas," Gwen Stefani, Blake Shelton

"I Don't Need It To Be Christmas At All," Matt Rogers

"I Wanna Be With You (On Christmas Day)," The National Parks

"Every Day Is Christmas," Colbie Caillat, Jason Reeves

"I Need You Tonight," Buddy Guy

"Forever," Mumford & Sons

"Love Is Not Enough," Ben Shannon

"So Long, London," Taylor Swift

"When You Say Nothing At All," Alison Kraus & Union Station

"I Heard the Bells on Christmas Morning," Echosmith

"Angel," Jack Johnson

"Ho Ho Ho And A Bottle of Rhum," Jimmy Buffett

"Joy," Iron & Wine

"Golden Hour," Kacey Musgraves

CHAPTER 1

Noelle
Monday

Joshua Morgenthal brandishes the glazed cinnamon roll at me as if it were a knife. The menace in his eyes is real, but the effect is undercut by the thin layer of frosting coating his whiskered chin. I lock eyes with him and inhale deeply, keeping my right palm outstretched.

"Mr. Morgenthal, hand over the pastry." I use my sternest librarian voice.

He shakes his head violently, sending a spray of crumbs spewing onto the colorful carpet.

"You've already had one Christmas roll," I point out. "And I specifically heard your husband tell you not to have any more sweets before he left."

I could hardly have missed it. Ryan's clear voice cut through the hushed library like a bell when he shouted the warning over his shoulder from the memoir and biography section on his way to the exit. The Mistletoe Mountain Public Library is usually a hive of activity—we're not one of those quiet libraries with the 'no talking' signs. But since the majority of the patrons this morning have their mouths stuffed with sweet rolls, we could be mistaken for one. I'll have piles of sticky, frosting-covered books to wipe down before closing.

I chide myself for the silent complaint. I shouldn't be so grouchy—or Grinchy. It is Christmas, after all. Well, Christmas in July, to be completely accurate. But in this town, there's no functional difference.

Mr. Morgenthal's gaze darts away from mine. He scans the lobby wildly as if searching for an escape route. At least he isn't going to bother denying the truth. Good call, what with the evidence all over his chin and the front of his shirt, not to mention the floor. When his bright brown eyes return to my face, he gives me a soulful look.

"Ah, come on, Noelle. Can't you look the other way? Let an old man have some sweetness in his drab, bitter life, why don't you?" He sticks out his glazed lip in a pout.

In point of fact, I *was* looking the other way when he grabbed the pastry. He waited until Roxie, the delivery driver, dropped off a big box of new mystery releases. Then he pounced. While I was focused on the latest book in the Maisy Farley mystery series, he slyly helped himself to another Christmas roll.

"Nice try. The roll. Now." I fist my left hand on my hip for emphasis.

We stare at each other. I really don't want to have to wrest the treat from his hand by force, but we both know I will if I have to. The seconds tick by. I ignore an itch on my nose. Finally, our dramatic standoff ends when he snorts in disgust and slaps the thing into my palm, sticky side down.

"Thank you," I say, adding lots of sugar to my voice to make up for depriving him of the real thing.

I get a grunt in return.

As I wrap the roll in a festive red napkin, then use a green one to work on my gunked-up hand, I give him a bemused look. "Are you trying to have a hyperglycemic episode?"

"No." He glares at me.

The whole town knows Mr. Morgenthal has diabetes. The whole town knows just about everything about everyone. Sweet Merry's, the bakery food truck, even has a sugar-free confection named for him.

"Why don't you have Ryan take you for a Josh's Jelly Roll after lunch?" I suggest.

He fake gags. "No way. Merry's making chocolate sponge this week."

"For the Jule-logs?"

He nods and wrinkles his nose. "I don't like the chocolate ones so much."

"You have my sympathies. But I still don't want you having a medical event in my library."

"Oh, it's your library, is it? And here I am laboring under the impression that this is a *public* library, paid for by my tax dollars. Anyway, I'm just trying to get into character."

"Into character for what?" I search my memory. I don't think he's in the cast of Mountainside Players' production of *It's A Wonderful Life,* but to be honest, I haven't been paying much attention. I'm not feeling very Christmassy this year.

"Didn't you hear? I'm playing Santa at the festival next weekend."

I give him a bewildered look. "You're July Santa?"

He chuckles. "Tell me about it. Who ever heard of a Jewish Santa? Ryan thinks I should say 'oy, oy, oy' instead of 'ho, ho, ho.'"

I shake my head, still confused. "No, you'll make a fabulous Santa. But why isn't Nick Jolly doing it? Nick always plays Santa at the Christmas in July festival. It's a tradition. He's Santa, and …."

As I trail off, he nods sadly. "Without Carol to play Mrs. Claus, I guess he doesn't want to do it this year."

My stomach twists and I start shaking as if I'm the one who's been mainlining sugar. I haven't thought about it, I realize with a guilty flush of heat in my cheeks. Nick's wife died last August. This will be his first Christmas in July without her. Even though he made it through the real Christmas last winter, this one's probably going to hit him harder.

I know it's hitting me harder. Carol Jolly was my best friend—had been ever since middle school, when she was still Carol Booker and thought the Christmas in July festival was the corniest, cringiest event in a town full of corny, cringy events. This isn't the most surprising take, given that we were eleven. But she maintained her healthy disdain for the summer Christmas festivities throughout high school and most of college.

Carol's views shifted radically, though, when she and Nick bought the Inn at Mistletoe Mountain right after they got married. She threw herself into the holidays, and they took on their roles as Mr. and Mrs. Claus even though they were only in their early twenties. This year, Christmas in July isn't going to be the same without her famous snowman ice cream cakes and her warm, lilting laughter. Nothing's the same without Carol.

I squeeze my eyes shut to hold back the tears that threaten to fall and feel a rough hand close over mine.

"It's okay to miss her," Mr. Morgenthal says in a gentle voice. "We all do."

I open my eyes and manage a wobbly smile. "I'm fine," I lie.

"You don't have to be, you know."

His empathy threatens to push me right over the edge. If I don't get a grip, I'm going to end up sobbing at the circulation desk. He either senses weakness or is trying to distract me from my grief because he reaches right over the desk and snatches the napkin-wrapped roll. Then he trots toward the front door with surprising speed and agility.

I sprint around the desk and race after him, yelling for him to stop in the name of blood sugar.

By the time I dodge a mother and son checking out the display of seed packets from our heirloom seed library and race outside, Mr. Morgenthal's halfway down the street.

"I'm calling Ryan!" I shout.

He glances over his shoulder and gives me a playful salute before he jaywalks across High Street, cackling as he goes. I skid to a stop and catch my breath to make good on my threat. I fish my phone out of the pocket of my dress and pull up Ryan's contact information.

After I leave a voicemail tattling on his sugar fiend of a husband, I wheel around to head back into the library and bump directly into a wall at full speed. Who put a wall in the middle of the sidewalk? As I bounce back from the impact, my brain catches up with my body and I realize I've just smacked into a broad, muscular chest covered in soft brushed cotton, not a wall.

"Did you just get outrun by an octogenarian?" a familiar voice asks in amusement.

I look up to see Nick Jolly's full lips curving into a broad smile, and I can sense he's holding back laughter—barely.

My face heats as I defend my athleticism or lack thereof. "One, Josh isn't an octogenarian. He's only seventy-eight. Two, he's faster than he looks. And three, he has the advantage of a sugar rush."

"If you say so."

I study his face. The hint of his smile lingers, but his gold-flecked hazel eyes are dull, devoid of their usual twinkle. My heart squeezes to see him this way.

"Hey…," I begin. Then I falter. I don't know what to say to him.

While I cast about for a way to bring up Carol, his loss, the summer Christmas festival—all of it—he asks, "Was it one of Merry's rolls that got Josh in trouble?"

"Um, yeah, it was."

He beams again, this time with fatherly pride. "She's a helluva baker." The smile wars with the sadness that radiates off him.

"She is." I could leave it at that, and maybe I should. But I don't. I swallow hard and add, "She gets it from her mom."

Carol loved to bake. Her creations weren't as fancy as Merry's are, but every cake, cookie, and pie she made was infused with warmth and emotion. She used to joke that a pinch of love was the secret ingredient in all her recipes. At least I thought it was a joke then. Now, I think she was on to something.

Nick's face tightens and the muscle in his left cheek twitches. "She does."

It's not even noon, but the July day promises to be a warm one. Nowhere near warm enough, though, to account for how sweaty I am as a result of this encounter. I should go. I've left the circulation desk unattended, which is less than ideal. And I've clearly upset him by mentioning Carol.

But, for some reason, instead of mumbling a goodbye, I say, "Josh told me he's filling in for you as Santa. Why?"

His expression shutters. He scans the street, looking for an escape. I can give him one. I mean, I *am* supposed to be inside, checking out materials and saving diabetics from themselves. But I don't take the easy way out. I owe Carol at least that much. So I watch his face and wait.

Finally, his shoulders slump and he sighs. "Noe."

I don't flinch at the old nickname, though I want to. He's the only one who's ever called me that. "What?"

"I can't. I can't do it. I miss her so much." He scrubs a hand over his face, and my heart seizes.

I reach out and wrap my hand around his upper arm. "I know," I whisper.

"You don't," he rasps. "You can't imagine."

"I don't have to imagine. She was my best friend, long before she even met you. I *do* know. I miss her every day."

"It's not the same."

He's right, of course. It's not. It's so much worse. Not because I think the way I loved my friend is remotely the same as the love the two of them shared, but because, at the very end, I lied to her. I can't say any of this to him, though.

It takes me several seconds to wrangle my emotions under some semblance of control. He stares at me, his gaze curious and steady, while I focus on my breath and try to hold back the tears that once again are building behind my eyes.

"Do you need help with the open house?" I finally manage, chickening out from saying anything more meaningful.

He swallows and shakes his head. "We're not having one."

"What do you mean you're not having one?"

The Inn at Mistletoe Mountain has been hosting an open house to kick off the Christmas in July festival for as long as I can remember. Since before Nick and Carol took it over.

"It's canceled this year."

I gape at him. "You can't just cancel it. I'm happy to lend a hand if you need help."

"I appreciate the offer, but I don't want a house full of people. Not this year."

Abdicating the role of Santa is bad enough. He can't get rid of the open house, too. The summer open house was, hands down, Carol's absolute favorite holiday event. My mind spins as I try to find the words to convince him not to do this. "Nick, it's a tradition, but it's more than that this year. It'll be a chance for the whole town to come together and celebrate Carol. Don't take that away from them. From me."

"Sorry, Noe."

And then it happens. A fat teardrop leaks from my left eye. I turn and flee ... running into the library. Behind me, I hear Nick calling my name, which only inspires me to pick up my pace. I dodge a pack of preschoolers trotting over to the gazebo with their music teacher to rehearse their song for the festival and run like a man trying to abscond with a frosted cinnamon roll.

CHAPTER 2

Nick

Noelle's stricken expression stays with me all morning, keeping me company on my circuit through town running the errands necessary to keep the inn going. Her horrified reaction was outsized, I tell myself, trying to eradicate the hollow feeling in the pit of my stomach.

I pull into the parking lot at the mill. It's just a party, I insist, as I back the truck into a spot near the door, hop out, and lower the tailgate. My inner monologue isn't working to dislodge the image of her bright green eyes filling with tears.

When I walk into the small retail shop attached to Marino and Sons Millworks, the tangy scent of baking bread fills my nostrils, and my stomach growls appreciatively.

"Morning, Nick," the flour-dusted young guy behind the counter says.

"Morning, Enzo."

The youngest of the Marino brothers wipes his hands on his apron and heads to the cash register. "We already pulled your order. Want me to give you a hand loading it?"

I almost say no, but I've got a twinge in my back from sleeping poorly and this kid's half my age. I feel ancient. I bet Josh Morgenthal could beat me in a foot race.

"Sure, that'd be great."

He rings up the purchases. "Your total comes to one hundred and fifty dollars."

I blink, and peel a third fifty from the roll of bills I already have out of my pocket. "Did your dad raise his prices?" A fifty percent increase is steep. I might need to start sourcing my flour from another supplier.

He cocks his head, puzzled. "No. The wholesale rate's the same as always. Fifty bucks for a fifty-pound bag."

I give him a confused look back. "I only ordered two."

"Ah, sure. But Merry called and said to add another bag. She needs it for the gingerbread houses. You know, for the open house."

My gut twists. I haven't gotten around to telling the girls that the open house is canceled. My daughters are going to make Noelle's reaction look mild.

"Oh. Right." I hand him the cash, and he studies me.

He looks like he wants to say something, but he doesn't. Instead, he holds out a receipt. I pocket it while he walks around to the front of the counter and stoops beside three large bags of flour waiting on a pallet. He hefts the top two bags onto his shoulder, and I grab the last one and follow him outside. We pile the sacks in the truck bed, then I close up the gate.

"Thanks for the help." I offer him a handshake.

"No problem." He pumps my hand and turns as if to leave, then turns back. "Is it true you're not playing Santa Claus this summer?"

The note of betrayal in his voice catches me off guard. Enzo's in his twenties. He hasn't stood in line to see Summer Santa in at least a dozen years, probably longer.

The sun's behind him, so I shade my eyes with my hand while I answer. "Yeah, not this summer."

"But—"

"Josh Morgenthal's going to stand in for me. He'll do a great job."

"But, he's not Santa. *You're* Santa."

I raise an eyebrow, but before I can break the news to him, he gives a sheepish laugh. "I didn't mean that how it sounded. It's just ... I can't remember a time when you didn't play Santa. You've been Santa my entire life. You're an institution, Nick. Our bookkeeper's daughter has been working on a note for you for two weeks. You remember Angelica?"

The name conjures up a shy five-year-old with long dark curls and big eyes. "Sure. Cute kid."

He frowns. "She's gonna know Mr. Morgenthal's not the real Santa."

I scratch my neck. "Look, Enzo. This is a bad year for me with ... everything. Josh'll be a perfectly serviceable Santa. And if Angelica notices that he's not me, just explain that the real Santa is extremely busy. Tell her he always has one of his helpers attend the summer festival."

"I guess." He's unconvinced. "Well, see you at the open house then."

I open my mouth, then I think better of it and snap it closed. He looks so dejected, I don't have the heart to break the news that the open house is canceled. Not now, at least.

He gives me a half-hearted wave and heads back inside.

As I put the truck in gear, Noelle's voice rings in my ears, telling me the open house is more than a tradition.

"Crud," I growl aloud.

I'm going to have to get out in front of this and let my daughters know there's not going to be an open house this year before they hear it from someone else.

I'M TOO LATE. I know it the instant I set foot in the kitchen. My three daughters sit at the big oak table, lined up by age—Holly, Ivy, and then Merry—wearing matching scowls.

"Uh-oh. What's the matter?" I figure playing dumb is my best option.

Holly isn't having it. She points a finger at me and uses her lawyer voice. "Is it true that you told Noelle Winters the summer open house is canceled?"

"Yes, but—"

Merry jumps in. "How *could* you?"

"Girls, you have to understand. I don't have—"

"Did you or did you not bow out of playing Summer Santa?" Holly demands.

I have the irrational urge to plead the Fifth. "Well—"

"Dad, you didn't!" Merry springs to her feet.

Quiet Ivy, who hasn't said a word, gapes at me, her mouth open and her eyes wide. And something inside me breaks. I drop into a chair across the table from them.

"I can't do it this year. I don't have it in me to be jolly and cheerful." Not while my heart is cracked in two, I add silently.

My confession diffuses their anger. The air changes, and Holly reaches over the table to squeeze my hand.

"Oh, Dad."

"I'm sorry you had to find out from Noelle. I should have told you."

Ivy agrees. "Yes, you should have. But we understand how hard this is for you. It's hard for all of us."

"Let us help you," Merry says, dropping into her seat again. "Don't back out of everything. Mom wouldn't want that."

"She'd hate it," Ivy informs me.

I study my daughters. Aside from their annoying habit of interrupting me, they're pretty great. Take-charge Holly, gentle Ivy, and bubbly Merry. Despite, or maybe because of, their disparate personalities, they're close, really close. They always have been. They're there for me and for each other. And when Carol was dying last summer, they were there for her.

"Do you think we can't handle the open house without Mom?" Holly wants to know. "Because we can. Besides, people will be happy to help if we ask them to. Noelle already offered."

I shake my head and have to clear my throat before I can speak. "No, of course not. I'm sure you're capable of pulling it off. The three of you can do anything you put your minds to. And Noelle told me the same thing about helping. But it's not the work that's daunting. It's facing Christmas in July without your mom."

One by one their gazes slide away from my face, and I know they're remembering our family summer Christmases. When you run the biggest inn in a town named Mistletoe Mountain, December is your busy season. The inn is booked solid from mid-November through early January, and every day is filled to bursting with seasonal activities, special meals, and themed crafts and games. As a result, in the Jolly family, our *real* Christmas celebration has always happened in July when the Mistletoe Mountain madness is slightly less all-consuming.

Somehow, through the hazy pain of missing Carol, I managed to forget that my daughters have a lifetime of summer Christmas memories. Of course, they're upset that I've canceled the holiday. The very reason why it's so painful to me is why it's so important to them. I'm a flipping moron.

Ivy speaks first. "Dad, please. We need to do this. For Mom, and for ourselves."

I swallow around the blasted lump in my throat. "Okay, do it. Have the open house, but I can't be a part of the prep work." My voice is gruff to my own ears.

They exchange careful looks and Ivy pours me a glass of ice water from the pitcher on the counter.

"Thanks," I tell her as she hands it to me.

"Are you sure?" Holly presses.

I take a long sip before answering. "I'm sure. Call Noelle. But leave me out of it."

"We don't need to call Noelle," Merry chirps. "We already called Aunt MJ."

I spew water and ice all over the table and sputter, "You what? *Why?*"

My sister, Mary Jane Field, is, to put it mildly, an agent of chaos. The girls start giggling, and Merry grabs a dish towel to wipe up the water.

"Relax, Dad. Aunt MJ isn't coming here."

"Whew, okay. You scared me there for a minute."

"Clearly," Holly says, arching an eyebrow.

They have no idea what a hot mess MJ can be. Her heart's in the right place. I think. But she leaves a trail of destruction and criminal charges in her wake.

"Is she even out of prison?" I ask.

"Yes, she and Uncle Bart were both released early for good behavior."

"Really? Well, they probably can't cross state lines without letting their parole officer know. So, I guess we're safe. But why on earth would you call her?"

"Because she runs a resort," Holly counters.

"She *ran* a resort. Ran it right into a pile of debt secured by a dangerous loan shark and left a mess for your cousins to clean up."

"Right," Merry agrees. "And they did clean it up. Rosemary, Sage, and Thyme have turned the Resort by the Sea around. It's thriving. And they manage it long distance. None of them even lives in New Jersey. Thyme keeps an eye on things from New York."

"I had no idea. Good for them."

"Didn't you talk to them at all when they were here last summer?" Ivy wonders.

Last summer. The funeral. It's a blur. A fuzzy Impressionist painting of pain and grief. My stomach churns at the memory of those dark days.

"If I did, I don't remember," I confess.

"Well, we did. And it was clear they have a lot of experience and some great ideas," Merry says.

"*And* they just happen to be at the Resort by the Sea this week and next for a family reunion," Ivy adds.

"Okay. And?" I pick up the glass and drink cautiously.

"And they jumped at the chance to help us out. Sage's husband had already arranged tickets to some golf tournament for the guys and Uncle Bart and Aunt MJ so the sisters could spend a few days alone together. Rosemary said they'd cancel their spa getaway and come up here instead," Holly says triumphantly.

"Great. Perfect." So long as Tropical Storm Mary Jane doesn't sweep through Mistletoe Mountain and destroy the whole town, this plan is fine by me. I really do love my sister —from a safe distance.

"The six of us will take care of everything," Ivy promises. "It'll be good for you, good for all of us. You'll see."

I can tell by the hope shining in my daughters' eyes that they think this plan is going to put their broken father back together. I hate to see them disappointed, but this idea is doomed to fail. I'm beyond saving. Still, it'll be good for them and the rest of the town to have the open house, so I muster up a smile, lean back with my glass of water, and let their conversation wash over me.

CHAPTER 3

Noelle
Tuesday

"Roll those hips," Griselda Alexander orders. She could be talking to the entire Hoop it Up fitness class, but she's staring directly at me. Into my soul, it seems.

"I'm trying" I grumble, catching my lip between my teeth as I concentrate on swiveling the weighted hoop around my midsection.

Rumor has it Griselda moved here to open Maple Twist Fitness after a successful career as a dancer both on Broadway and on tours for some big-name musical acts. That's the story, but I have a growing suspicion she actually retired from the military—specifically, as a boot camp instructor. I keep this to myself. In part, because she terrifies me, and, in part, because she's a huge supporter of the library. She personally donated all the funds to cover the remodeled children's wing last year.

"Winters, shake your booty!" she barks, putting to rest the question of whether her instructions are meant for me or everyone.

Sweat blooms on my forehead as several sets of eyes shift from the mirrored wall to me, watching with open interest my efforts to shake my booty. Someone in the back row titters, and I grit my teeth. I'm about to concede defeat, roll my hoop off the floor, and hang it on one of the pegs on the wall when I glimpse Nick through the studio's front window.

He's on the other side of the street, sprinting and casting wild backward glances over his shoulder as if he's being chased. He waits for a break in traffic, then bolts across the street and bursts through the doors into the studio. He screeches to a halt in the doorway, panting hard.

Griselda glares at him. "Class started ten minutes ago, Jolly." Then she points at me. "Move over and make room for him."

"Sorry." He maneuvers through the sea of gyrating bodies, grabs a hoop, and squeezes into the spot I've made next to me.

"I didn't know you take this class," I say out of the side of my mouth as he steps into the hoop.

"I don't," he whispers back. "I prefer the pole dancing class."

I snicker, and he gives me a confused look.

"Oh. You're serious."

"It's a great workout. You should try it."

Yeah, right. I'll be lucky if Griselda doesn't bust me back down to the beginners' Bollywood dance class, given my insufficient undulating skills. I can't imagine making any moves that would pass muster while hanging upside down from a pole. I *am* curious to see Nick doing it, though. My cheeks heat at the thought and I hurriedly clear my throat.

"So why are you here?"

"Hiding."

Before I can ask who he's hiding from, Griselda frowns and jabs her finger toward our corner. "Move your hips, not your lips."

I smother a giggle, and Nick covers his laugh with a cough.

I grit my teeth and flail my way through the remaining thirty-five minutes of class, acutely aware of Nick standing to my left. When class is over, I'm prepared to flee, but Nick stretches his hands out. "Give me your hoop. I'll return it for you."

"Thanks."

His fingers brush against mine as I hand him the hula hoop, and electricity sparks between us. I tell myself it's static because I have dry skin and not his effect on me. Still, I loiter in the hallway, putting my shoes on in slow motion so I can say a proper goodbye to him and take another crack at trying to convince him to celebrate summer Christmas.

While I'm waiting, Griselda sashays over to me with a wide smile. It's wild how much nicer she is outside of class.

"Hey, I want to let you know I'm having a large package sent to the library."

Why wouldn't she have it delivered here or to her house? I

give her a curious look and then shrug. "Okay. Do you need me to bring it over for you?"

"No, no, it's for you. Well, for the library. I was reading an article that said pretend play is so important for young children and they're not getting enough of it now with all the screens. So, I ordered a set of puppets and a puppet theater stage for the children's wing."

"Oh, that's great. Kids love puppets."

"They do, right?"

"They do," I assure her. "It's really thoughtful, and I'm sure it'll get a lot of use. Thanks."

She waves a hand. "Don't mention it."

Just then, Nick returns from the equipment corner, wiping the sweat from his neck with a towel. "Another great class, Grizzy," he tells her.

"Grizzy?" I manage to suppress my laugh.

She turns to me. "You know, he could help with your hip thrusts."

"What?" I choke.

"Nick. He could show you how to get your hips thrusting. He's good at that."

"Thanks," I say weakly, hoping that the floor will open up a hole to swallow me.

No such luck. But for an instant, I think it swallowed Nick because he drops flat on his belly. Griselda and I exchange a bewildered look.

"Nick, are you—?"

"Shh." As he shushes me, he army crawls on his elbows out of view of the window.

Noise out on the sidewalk catches my attention, and I turn to see Nick's daughters and three other young women laughing and talking as they walk down the street. They stop directly in front of the fitness studio's front door, and Merry gestures toward the sign.

"Are you hiding from your daughters?" I ask Nick's departing back.

He doesn't answer as he rolls into a storage closet that happens to be ajar. He eases the door shut behind him, and Griselda shakes her head. She's as confused as I am.

The door opens, and the women troop inside.

"Griselda," Holly says, "I want you to meet my cousins, Rosemary, Sage, and Thyme Field."

"What, no Parsley?" The fitness instructor cracks, and I can tell by the women's faces that it's not the first or even thousandth time they've heard that joke.

"Parsley's the cat," the blonde says. "I'm Rosemary."

"This is Griselda Alexander," Holly continues. "She's the town's fantastic fitness diva."

Griselda smiles and doesn't bother to be humble. "How nice that your cousins are visiting."

"Yeah, they're here to help with the Christmas in July open house. We had to stop in because Thyme is a yoga and Pilates instructor and personal trainer in New York City."

Griselda eyes the willowy brunette who Holly's pointing to. Judging by her expression, she's giving Thyme a quick professional assessment. "Where did you train?"

"Oh, I was a psychology major in college, and I read this study about how yoga and meditation can help so much with stress. So I took a yoga class, mainly out of curiosity. I loved it, so after a while, I got my instructor's certificate. Just for fun, really. Eventually, I started taking Pilates, and one thing led to another."

Griselda meets this pat explanation with an arched eyebrow. "Really? You fell into a career as a personal trainer?"

The middle sister, Sage, pipes up. "Well, Thyme's leaving out the part where our parents owed a loan shark a half-million dollars, put up the family business as collateral, and skipped town. So the three of us had to find a way to make a lot of money, fast. Thyme dropped out and started working as a personal fitness instructor for a very famous media mogul. Like, you'd know her name."

Thyme gives her sister a look before chirping, "*Anyway,* this studio looks like so much fun. My cousins were telling me you offer loads of unusual classes. I'd love to do one while we're in town if I have time."

Holly and Rosemary say in unison, "We won't."

I peg Rosemary as the eldest sister of the cousins.

"We're going to be very busy," Holly explains.

Merry frowns. "I think Thyme knows how much goes into event planning, Holly. I mean, she *is* a hospitality professional."

Ivy turns to us, "Thyme basically runs the Resort by the Sea, the inn their parents handed over to them. The resort's in New Jersey, so she oversees things from Manhattan."

"That's convenient," I say.

"Oh my goodness," Ivy's eyes go wide. "We didn't introduce you. I'm so sorry. This is Noelle Winters. She's our town librarian. And she was Mom's best friend." At the mention of Carol, everyone's smile dims a bit.

"She's good friends with Dad, too," Merry adds.

While I'm wondering exactly what she means by *that*, Griselda starts yapping.

"Yes, she and your father were just—"

Before Griselda can dime Nick out for hiding in the closet, I bring my tennis shoe-clad foot down on her bare one.

"Ouch! Winters!" she barks.

"Oh, I'm sorry, Griselda. I'm such a klutz." I fake a sheepish smile.

"Tell me something new," she grumbles.

I ignore that and turn back to the visitors. "I'm so glad you're here to help your cousins." Then I glance at Holly, Ivy, and Merry. "My offer stands. If you need anything, please let me know."

"We will," Holly promises. "But, between the six of us, we should have it covered."

Ivy jumps in. "Oh, but you should come over to the inn for afternoon tea one day this week, Noelle. Rosemary's husband is a homicide detective in Los Angeles. We know how you love murder mysteries. She could probably tell you some wild stories."

My eyes light up. "Really?"

Sage laughs. "Not just Rosie. We've all been involved in some … crime dramas."

The Field sisters exchange knowing looks.

"Oooh, I'm intrigued."

"That settles it. Come over for tea tomorrow morning," Merry says.

"It's a date."

The women say their goodbyes to Griselda and sweep back outside in a cloud of chatter.

The closet door creaks open and Nick peeks through the opening.

"The coast is clear," I tell him.

He steps out into the hallway and blinks at the light. "Thanks."

"Why are you hiding from your daughters?"

"It's a long story. Why don't I tell you over a beverage? You want to join us, Grizzy?"

"Appreciate the offer. But I can't. My Rump Shaker class starts in twenty minutes."

"Thanks again for the puppets," I tell her.

"Don't mention it. Remember, Noelle, you have to gyrate!"

Nick holds the door open for me, and Griselda's shout follows us out onto the pavement.

"Coffee?" I propose.

He considers, then shakes his head. "No, the girls will probably pop into the Snowflake so their cousins can meet Delphina. Why don't we go to Santa's Cellar?"

Nope. No way am I having drinks with my dead best friend's husband at the romantic wine bar where he proposed to her. Sure, that was well over a quarter century ago, but it still feels wrong.

"Rudy's is closer," I say.

It *is* closer. But the Tipsy Turnip and the North Pole Social Club are closer still. They're right on the town square while Rudy's Roadhouse is on the very edge of town, just barely walkable. But unlike the others, Rudy's is also known for its rowdy crowd and a distinctly unromantic atmosphere. Think sticky floors and an alt-rock playlist rather than votive candles and soft instrumental music.

He quirks an eyebrow but doesn't argue. After a moment, he shrugs. "Sure, okay. Rudy's it is."

We cross the street and head down the hill to the roadhouse.

CHAPTER 4

Nick

I'm sweating by the time we reach Rudy's. The late afternoon sun beats down on us as we traipse down the hill. I give Noelle a sidelong glance, but she doesn't seem bothered by the heat. What was I thinking, suggesting Santa's Cellar? Rudy's, despite the walk, is a better choice.

I push open the door and usher her ahead of me into the cool interior, where we're greeted by a blast of air conditioning. The dim bar is about half full with happy hour patrons and two guys camped out with a backgammon board in a corner booth. Chip and Jamal are both fellow Santas—winter Santas. Although I've historically handled Christmas in July duties myself, there's a whole roster of Santa Clauses for the winter holidays. I could have asked any one of them to pinch hit next week, but Josh Morgenthal offered. And, truth be told, the Santa Claus Crew gossips worse than a pack of middle-school girls. I didn't want word to get around the Kris Kringle whisper network. That would have only brought a steady stream of St. Nicks trying to change my mind.

So when we pass by Jamal and Chip's table, I smile and nod a greeting but don't stop to talk. I lead Noelle to a two-top near the kitchen.

"Is this okay?"

"Sure." She perches on the high stool and takes the laminated menu from the holder on the table. "Share a serving of poutine?" she asks without so much as glancing at the menu.

I hide a smile. Noelle always did like french fries. "Sounds good."

Rudy's wife strolls over to take our order, plucking a stubby pencil from behind her ear. "Hi, Nick. Hey, Noelle."

"Hi, Tammy," we say in unison.

"What's it going to be?"

"We'll split an order of poutine," Noelle tells her.

"What drafts are on special for happy hour?" I ask.

Tammy gives me the stink eye. "Are you really going to make me rattle off fifteen beers when we both know you're going to order a Frosty Ale like always?"

She has a point. "Fair. I'll have a Frosty Ale."

"Big one or a little one?"

"We're walking," I tell her. "Make it a big one."

"You got it. What about you, Noelle? Peppermint martinis are on special."

"Tempting. But I do love my fries with wine. How about a glass of Mistletoe Merlot?"

"You got it."

She sticks the pencil back behind her ear and leaves to put in our order.

Across the table, Noelle cocks her head. "So how do you get away with calling Griselda 'Grizzy'? I've always thought of her more like a *grizzly,* but I'd never dare to say it to her face."

"She's got a gruff exterior but she's a marshmallow on the inside."

"I know," Noelle confesses. "She's the library's biggest donor."

"Really? Didn't expect that."

"She financed the addition of the children's wing. She seems to have a special fondness for kids. Kind of strange that she doesn't have any of her own."

I shake my head. "I don't know that she particularly likes kids. It's probably more that she didn't have much of a childhood herself. Gris was a stage kid. She was in her first Broadway show when she was seven. Her parents pulled her out of school, and she had tutors on set and when she toured. She's been working more or less full-time since second grade. She missed out on all the typical kid experiences."

Her green eyes are sad. "I had no idea." Then she throws me a puzzled look. "How do you know all this?"

"When Carol got too sick to really exercise, she still wanted to do something physical to feel embodied. Gris came to the house to do restorative yoga sessions with her pretty much every day right up until the end. The three of us ended up talking a lot."

"Oh." A heavy silence falls over the table. "I didn't know," she says slowly.

She wouldn't, because at the very end, Noelle disappeared. Carol tried to pretend that her best friend abandoning her as she was dying didn't hurt, but I could tell it gutted her. The memory of her bewilderment at the betrayal makes my heart pound, and I fist my hands to keep myself from lashing out at Noelle after all this time.

As if she's reading my mind, she says, "I wasn't around as much as I should have been at the end."

"It's hard," I tell her. "Some people can't handle death." It's a BS excuse, but I give it to her anyway.

She shakes her head. "No. That's not it. The last time I saw Carol, I came over to wash her hair and paint her nails." She pauses and takes a shaky breath. "She asked me to do something for her after she died. I didn't want to tell her no. I mean, who turns down their dying best friend's last wish?"

This is news to me. I stare at her. "What did she ask you to do?"

"It's private."

"Did you do it?" I press.

She sighs heavily but holds my gaze. "I told her I couldn't. And after that, I couldn't face her."

Her expression closes, and I know this topic's off-limits. Before I can try to find another way in, Tammy's back with our drinks.

"Waters are coming. I'll bring them out with the fries."

"Cheers," Noelle says in a low voice.

I don't think either one of us feels like clinking glasses. I'm consumed with curiosity about what Carol asked her, but she's right. It's not my place to know.

"I regret not being honest with her, Nick. If I had, I wouldn't have ghosted her because I felt guilty."

Her voice trembles, and the anguish in her eyes drains the anger from my body. I reach across the table and cover her hand with mine.

"Death's hard, Noe. Grieving's hard. I should know, I almost deprived my daughters of the open house. And that would have been the wrong thing to do."

She manages a wan smile and sips her wine. "I'm glad you changed your mind."

"I didn't really have a choice after you called and told them."

"Sorry," she interrupts with a sheepish shrug that makes it clear she's not one bit sorry.

I go on. "They reached out to my nieces, and, well, you saw them. Combined, they're a force to be reckoned with. They'll have no problem running the show."

"It's good you've got so much help."

I shake my head. "I'm going to go to my fishing cabin for the rest of the week."

She gives me a disappointed look. "Nick, you can't hide from this."

She's one to talk. Didn't she just admit she hid from Carol when she was dying? I want to shoot back. I take a long swig of the cold beer instead.

"No one's going to miss me with all that activity. Besides, I haven't been to the cabin yet this summer. I need to air it out and chase the spiders away. Don't worry, I'll show up when all the work is done—like a blister."

She twists her mouth but doesn't argue.

Tammy's back. Noelle slips her hand free as an enormous tray of french fries covered in gravy and cheese curds thunks down on the middle of the table. A barback trails behind her with two sweating glasses of ice water. He slides them onto a pair of cardboard coasters on the table.

"Bon appetit," Tammy says over her shoulder, walking away.

A guy playing pool pauses his game to feed money into the jukebox and a loud rock anthem blares. I watch as Noelle pops a smothered fry into her mouth and marvel at the fact that I'm sitting across a table from her.

Noelle Winters is the whole reason I came to Mistletoe Mountain in the first place. I never would have met Carol if I hadn't fallen for Noelle in London almost thirty years ago.

We were college juniors, both doing internships the summer before our senior year. She was working with the archivists at the British Library. I was interning at Claridge's, the famous hotel, as part of my hospitality management major. MJ and her husband had just bought the Resort at the Sea, and the plan was for me to get some hands-on experience before I graduated, then go to work for my older sister and Bart.

I met Noelle at the launderette around the corner from the flat I was subletting. She was parked on a folding chair reading Sherlock Holmes while her clothes dried. I reached into my pocket and pulled out a fist full of change for the machine. As I sorted through the quarters looking for the distinctive heptagon shape of the fifty-pence pieces I needed, she closed her book, crossed the room, and offered me a handful of the coins.

"Here. I'm almost done."

I looked up, fell into those green eyes, and didn't come up for air all summer. We'd meet after work for takeaway curries, cheap wine, and long walks through narrow cobblestone streets steeped in history and drama. We were broke, starry-eyed, and in love. I was, at least.

But when it came time to return to the States for our senior year, she didn't. The library offered her a position and helped her transfer to Oxford for her final year with a promise to hook her up with the prestigious Bodleian Library traineeship after that. It was a once-in-a-lifetime opportunity, too good to pass up. I understood. Of course, I did.

We scraped up the money to take the Chunnel to Paris for our last weekend before I flew back home. It was crowded, noisy, and pure romance. I snapped a picture of her on the Pont au Double bridge over the Seine. She's standing with Notre Dame behind her, the wind lifting her long, red hair from her shoulders, her smile wide, and her arms thrown open as if she was giving the entire City of Lights a hug.

And that was that.

Maybe in today's world we'd keep in touch. But in a time before texts, video chats, and social media, we didn't. Email wasn't even really a thing yet. We wrote a few airmail letters, had one obscenely expensive phone call, and then fizzled. I tucked away the memory of the green-eyed redhead who loved Agatha Christie, puzzles, and maple syrup over her ice cream and moved on.

As my graduation approached, I started looking for a job in the tourist industry. MJ and Bart were still getting the Resort by the Sea off the ground, and it was slow going. MJ was pregnant with Rosemary, and money was tight. We agreed I'd get some more industry experience under my belt before they brought me onboard. Remembering the stories Noelle used to tell about her holiday wonderland of a hometown, I sent a resume to the Inn at Mistletoe Mountain on a whim.

The proprietor called and offered me a job managing the inn over the phone. After fifty-seven Vermont winters, he and his wife were ready to pack it up and retire to Florida. We agreed to a one-year trial, then, if we both wanted to proceed, I'd buy the inn from him.

I loaded my clothes and books into the back of my beat-up Rabbit and headed north two days after I got my diploma. Six weeks after I arrived in town, I met a witty, vivacious blonde at the Christmas in July festival, fell head over heels, and never looked back.

Carol and I got engaged eighteen months later. When we started planning the wedding, she tracked down her childhood bestie, who was doing graduate work in Italy, and asked her to be her maid of honor. The night Noelle Winters walked through the door of the inn for our engagement party was like a punch to my gut.

"Penny for your thoughts." Noelle's clear voice cuts through the noise and penetrates my thoughts.

"That'll cost you at least fifty pence," I tell her, reaching for a goopy french fry.

Her eyes go wide and her face softens, and I know she's remembering the launderette, too.

We didn't hide the fact that we knew each other from Carol. But we both shrugged off our past as a summer fling, nothing more. No big deal. It was ancient history then, and it's ancient history now. Someone needs to tell my racing heart that.

CHAPTER 5

Noelle
Wednesday

I'm so engrossed in the climax of the new mystery that I don't hear the footsteps approaching. Just as the sleuth is about to reveal how she unmasked the killer, my chair whirls around in a circle, and I gasp.

I jerk my head up to see Farah, the high school student working with me this summer, grinning. "You're going to be late for your appointment."

I stick a quitter strip between the pages to mark my place and glance at my watch. "Shoot. I am."

"Isn't tea supposed to be in the afternoon?"

As I grab my purse and shove my book and phone into it, I explain. "You're thinking of afternoon tea. We're actually having elevenses," I tell her.

"Like the hobbits?"

I laugh. "Well, yes, but also like the British. It's a late morning snack. It's not as fancy as afternoon tea, which, in turn, is not as fancy as high tea."

Farah gives me a look. "The Brits really like their tea, huh?"

"They really do," I agree. "Are you sure you'll be okay handling the desk alone and maybe helping set up the puppet theater if you get a chance?"

"Piece of cake," she assures me. "Ooh, if there's cake, will you bring me back a slice?"

"Definitely," I promise before hurrying out of the building.

I slip my sunglasses on as I speed-walk the block and a half to the Inn at Mistletoe Mountain. I break into a jog as the bell in the old courthouse building chimes the hour. On the ninth chime, I race up the stairs and jab at the doorbell. While I wait for someone to answer it, I try to decide whether I'm hoping to run into Nick or not.

I'm jittery and off-balance. Our college romance burned bright and hot, as such things tend to do. But it flared out fast, and once he and Carol got together, I placed our brief romance firmly in the past and Nick even more firmly in the friend zone. Of course he fell in love with Carol. Who wouldn't?

They were one of those couples who just glowed. They belonged together. But last night, when he brought up the way we met in London, a wave of memories that I've been holding back for more than a quarter century crashed over me. And I haven't been able to catch my breath since.

Ivy opens the grand wooden doors and waves me inside with a bright grin.

"Right on time." She leans over and gives me a soft hug. "I hope tea in the kitchen is okay."

"It's perfect. Elevenses isn't very formal," I remind her.

Her grin broadens. "That's right, you're the one who turned Mom on to elevenses in the first place."

"She was pregnant with Holly." I laugh at the memory.

Carol was ravenous during her second trimester, and the hours between breakfast and lunch seemed interminable. So we made it a habit to meet up for an eleven o'clock snack and a cup of tea. Herbal for her, and Lady Grey for me.

As Ivy leads me to the kitchen, I notice that the parlor and dining room aren't yet decorated for Christmas in July and suppress a frown. The girls have tons to do in the next few days. Nick really ought to stick around and help them.

"Did your dad already leave for the fishing cabin?" I ask.

"Yeah, you just missed him."

I ignore the flash of disappointment that runs through me.

"Listen, if you need another pair of hands—"

She waves me off. "I know we're a little behind, but there are six of us. It'll be a breeze."

"I'm here. You might as well put me to work."

She relents. "We're going to go up to the attic after tea to bring down the decorations, if you want to help with that."

"I'd love to." I need to do something to help, seeing I'm the one who tattled on Nick to his daughters.

We traipse into the light-filled kitchen, and I'm greeted by a chorus of voices.

I dig into my purse, pull out a small wooden box, and place it on the counter. "To have a proper elevenses, we need some authentic English tea."

Ivy, Holly, and Merry dart over to the box, oohing over the assortment of sachets.

As they paw through the teas, I explain to their cousins, "I lived in England for a while in my early twenties. I got hooked on the good stuff."

Sage gasps and points to the corner of the book peeking out from the top of my bag. "Is that the new Maisy Farley mystery?"

"It sure is."

Her face falls. "I'm on the holds list for a copy at my library back home. But it's going to be a while. I'm number forty-four."

"Noelle can hook you up," Holly tells her.

She should know. I've been feeding her books since before she could tie her own shoes.

"Really?"

I flash a mischievous grin and pull the book out of my bag. "I have maybe fifteen pages left to read. If you ladies don't mind if I read them now, I'll leave this book with you."

Sage's eyes widen. "Isn't there a holds list?"

"I haven't actually shelved it yet," I confess. "It's one of the perks of being a librarian. Growing up, I told my mom librarians had the best job because they could read all the books for free. She worriedly asked me if I understood how libraries worked."

I pause while they giggle, then go on, "But, it turns out, my position *does* have some privileges. I'll be happy to let you read it before I put it into circulation. You just have to promise not to lose it—or I'll have to fine myself."

This isn't strictly true. I don't assess fines for overdue or lost materials. But that's my little secret.

She claps her hands like a little girl. "I promise."

"Okay, I'll pop into the parlor and zip through this last chapter."

"What kind of tea do you want?" Holly calls after me.

Ivy answers for me. "She wants Lady Earl Grey with steamed oat milk and a dash of vanilla."

I pause in the doorway and turn to blink at her in surprise.

"Lady London Fog. It's your favorite," she declares.

She's right, and the fact she knows this makes my heart swell in my chest. Since when am I this sentimental? I shake my head at myself, smile back at her, and hurry out of the kitchen with a lump in my throat.

I perch in the window seat, balance the book on my knees, and zip through the denouement and epilogue. I close the book with a satisfied flourish and head back into the kitchen.

I place the book on the table in front of Sage and whisper, "She's all yours."

"Perfect timing," Merry chirps, handing me a porcelain teacup.

I take a seat at the big oak table and settle against one of the striped cushions Carol made the year she taught herself how to use the old sewing machine in the parlor. I cup my hands around the tea and inhale the fragrant steam. Mixed with the scents of bergamot, citrus, and lavender that I expect, I smell strong roasted coffee. I wrinkle my forehead and turn to my right.

"Are you drinking coffee?" I say to Holly.

"Guilty as charged," she admits, "but I'm not the only one."

Rosemary raises a hand. "I just can't with the tea. I'm a coffee girl."

"I understand," I tell her. "After England, I entered a master's program at the University of Bologna in Ravenna and, let me tell you, there's *nothing* like a good Italian espresso."

Rosemary's eyes light up and she starts gushing about an authentic Italian coffee bar near her home.

"Do you go there with your homicide detective?" I ask as I reach for a cucumber and olive sandwich.

Merry laughs. "Smooth segue, Noelle."

I shrug unapologetically. "I really am a mystery and true crime junkie. Does your husband talk about his work a lot?"

"Not often," Rosemary says. "He doesn't like to bring that home with him."

"Oh." I feel my shoulders droop.

"But … we met because I was the prime suspect in a murder investigation."

My eyes widen. "Really?"

"Yep. I was working as a private chef for a truly nasty movie star. Someone offed her, and I had to find the real killer before the cops pinned it on me."

"*You* found the real murderer?"

"Sure did." She pops a mini-quiche into her mouth.

Thyme clears her throat noisily.

Rosemary shoots her a look and amends, "Fine. Technically, the police did. But I helped."

"You did help," Sage allows before leaning across the table to say, "I also caught a murderer."

"You didn't."

"I did. And so did Thyme."

Thyme shakes her head. "Not exactly. I *stopped* a murder."

"Details, details." Sage waves a hand.

"And don't even *ask* about our weddings," Rosemary says.

"Tell me everything," I demand.

They talk over one another in a rush. One wild story after another spills from their lips while I sip my tea and nibble on the goodies.

LISTENING TO THE COUSINS' stories is like binge watching an entire season of a detective series. Before I know it, the grandfather clock in the parlor is chiming the hour again.

At exactly noon, Holly pushes back her chair and brushes the crumbs from her fingers. "All right, are we ready to tackle the attic?"

The rest of us rise more slowly, reluctant to leave the easy camaraderie of the table.

"I'll walk you out," Merry offers, turning to me.

"No, no. I'll help you bring the decorations down. I used to help your mom with this every year, you know."

Sadness falls over the room like a heavy blanket at the mention of Carol. Anger flares in my chest at Nick. He shouldn't have left his daughters to do this without him—cousins or no cousins.

But Holly lifts her chin, sets her mouth in a thin, determined line and says, "That'd be great. You probably know where things go even better than we do."

I probably do, I think, as we file through the grand parlor

and sitting room to the sweeping spiral staircase and then down the long second floor hall, past eight bedroom doors that will all be decorated with wreaths. At the end of the hall, a second, slightly less grand staircase leads to the attic.

We mount the stairs and I push the door open. Stuffy, hot air hits me in the face. Beads of sweat pop out on my forehead as Holly beelines toward the row of shelves along the wall that holds the summer Christmas decorations.

The Jollys fan out and start grabbing boxes, passing them assembly-line style toward their cousins near the stairs. Merry hands me a box and I scan the label. Carol's distinctive handwriting is like a blow to my heart.

"Your nutcrackers are in here."

Merry gives me a sad smile. "Some of them."

Carol adored nutcrackers. Her delight turned out to be her downfall once everyone in town realized her obsession. After a few years, she had dozens and dozens of nutcrackers—enough to take on any Rat King and his army. She graciously displayed every single one during the Christmas in July open house. But she held back a handful of especially meaningful ones to put out in the family's private living quarters. This is the box I clutch. It's labeled *Family Nutcrackers.*

"This one goes to your family room," I tell them. "Should I take it down?"

"Might as well," Holly says over her shoulder. "Just plop it in the family room. We'll decorate in there once the guest areas are done."

I gingerly carry the carton downstairs and through the kitchen to the wing at the back of the house where the Jolly family has a space apart from their paying guests. The girls have enough on their plate with all the decorating in the front of the building, so I decide to at least get started in here by setting up the nutcrackers. I remove the lid and gently dig through the box.

The very first nutcracker I see is the Nancy Drew nutcracker I got for Carol the year Merry was born. The girl detective wears a festive holiday dress and peers through a magnifying glass. I place it on top of the bookcase and pull out the next box. An Old World Saint Nicholas with a merry smile goes on the shelf next to Nancy Drew.

I'm reaching for a classic toy soldier when my eye snags on a thick linen envelope nestled between a pair of clear boxes. I draw it out from the storage container and blink down at my name. *Please deliver to Noelle Winters* is typed on the front of the envelope. And it does appear to be *typed*. With a typewriter. The letters are raised. I rub my thumb over them and frown.

Holly appears in the doorway. "Hey, thanks for getting started setting these up."

I glance up at her. "Of course."

"What's that?" She gestures toward the envelope.

"I don't know. It was in the box."

I pass it to her. She draws her eyebrows together. "How'd this get in there? Who's it from?"

"Your mom?" I suggest.

She shakes her head. "I don't think so. Mom was in the hospital in Burlington when we packed up this room. Dad called and asked us to take care of it before he brought her home. We had to take down the Christmas tree and put away the decorations to make room for the … hospital bed." She clears her throat.

I choke back tears. When Carol realized she only had weeks left, she insisted on having hospice care at home. She wanted to die in the place she loved surrounded by the people she loved.

Holly's right. I remember. This room wasn't decorated when Carol came home. The last time I saw her—the day she asked me if I still had feelings for her husband—I was perched on the edge of a narrow bed in this very room, pressing a cold cloth against her fevered forehead.

"Noelle, do you still care for him?" Carol's voice was thin and raspy.

I was confused. "Who?"

"Nick."

She no sooner got his name out than her frail frame was wracked by a fit of violent, shuddering coughs. When she collapsed back against the pillow, I picked up her water glass with shaking hands and guided the straw to her lips.

"Here, take a sip."

She tried to bat it away. "Noelle? Did you hear me?"

I waited until she drank, then I set the glass aside and stared into her tired blue eyes. "I heard you. Of course not. That was decades ago. Water under the bridge. Ancient history."

She grabbed my wrist with surprising strength, cutting off my steady stream of lies. "Stop."

"Nick loves *you*, Carol."

She gave me a sad smile. "I know. And I love him. But he's

not going to be okay when I'm gone. He's going to need someone to help him through it."

"You're not going anywhere. You're going to beat this," I told her fiercely.

My best friend held my gaze as she shook her head slowly. "No, Noelle. I'm not. I'm dying. I'm dying, and I love you, and I love Nick. So if you can be there for each other after I'm gone, you should. It's what I want."

I had to clear my throat several times to choke the words out. "I'll be there for Nick and your girls because I love you, and because I love them. All of them. As a friend. Okay? That's all I am. A friend."

She held my gaze for a moment longer and something like disappointment filled her eyes. Then a shadow crossed her face as her eyelids fluttered closed. Once she was soundly sleeping, I covered her with a thin blanket and fled the house like I was being chased.

I figured I'd give her a few days, let the awkwardness of that conversation fade, and then things would be back to normal between us. Or as close to normal as they could be given the situation. But I misjudged how much time we had. The next time I stepped foot inside the inn was for the celebration of life after her burial service.

"Earth to Noelle!"

The sickening memory fades as I jerk myself back to the present. Holly's waving a paper an inch in front of my nose.

"Sorry." I manage shakily. "Lost in thought."

"Clearly." She thrusts the paper into my hands. "Look! It's a map. And a riddle. Someone put together a scavenger hunt for you!"

My heartache over the memory of that last conversation with Carol doesn't go away. It doesn't even fade. But it *does* slide over to make room for the excitement that stirs in me as I stare down at the map of Mistletoe Mountain and a small envelope marked *Clue No. 1*.

Holly yells for the others to get in here, and they all crowd around, urging me to open the clue. I slit the envelope open with my fingernail, remove a folded note card, and scan the typed note.

"Well? What's it say?" Rosemary demands.

I read it aloud: *'Your first clue isn't difficult. The land of the sweets has many treats. Go to the place where you'll find a strong one.'*

Merry claps her hands. "How fun! Noelle, you have your very own holiday mystery!"

I'm still staring down at the clue, wheels turning. When I look up, I can't hide my grin. "Looks that way. I wish you girls could solve it with me, but—"

Sage groans. "But we have our hands full with the open house prep."

"We'll live vicariously through you," Ivy assures me. "Be sure to report back."

I tuck the envelope away in my purse and promise to do exactly that.

CHAPTER 6

Nick

The sun glints off the lake as my truck bumps along the unpaved access road that leads to the fishing cabin. I'm almost to the turnoff at the bottom of what I charitably call my driveway when I spot Enrique Morales flagging me down from the path out of the woods. I roll to a stop and lower my window.

Enrique's my closest neighbor up here, although his cabin is a good quarter mile from mine. So we don't exactly see a lot of each other unless we run into each other in town. He taught middle school social studies in Brooklyn for twenty-five years. When he retired six years ago, he moved up here and developed a love for skiing. Mistletoe Mountain doesn't have a big ski resort of its own. Folks head over to one of the more established spots for serious skiing. But our county park has a couple slopes and a rustic ski lodge. Enrique—who swore he'd never work with kids again after he retired—teamed up with the school district to run an after-school ski club in season.

He's not coming from the direction of his property. The footpath he's on leads down from the ski lodge. I lean out to greet him.

"Morning."

"Morning, Nick," he returns the greeting, but his expression is pinched.

"Everything okay, Enrique?"

"Not sure. When I was walking Bear this morning, he kept pulling in the direction of the lodge. You know how retrievers are, though. I figured he was on a scent. But he was really insistent, barking up a storm. He dug his heels in when I tried to go the other direction. So we walked up that way. And, well, it looks like someone broke into the lodge."

"Crap," I mutter under my breath. "You sure?"

"Seems that way. One of the windows is busted. I took a peek inside. The furniture's been moved around. I took Bear back to my place and grabbed the key to the lodge."

"You didn't go in there by yourself, did you?"

He shakes his head. "I was just starting back up the mountain when I heard your truck. Feel like coming along?"

Not really, but I'm not about to let him go up there alone.

"Sure," I tell him. "Hop in."

"Appreciate it, Nick."

I push open the passenger door and he climbs in. Then I execute a tight U-turn and head back out to the road. We drive in silence until we reach the road up to the lodge. About three quarters of the way up the hill, I pull into a small, unpaved parking area in front of the trailhead that leads down to the meadow. I nudge the nose of the truck under the low-hanging branches of a huge white pine, out of the line of sight from the front of the lodge.

"Let's approach on foot," I suggest. "There's no need to announce our arrival in case someone's still in there."

I kill the engine, and we hop out of the truck. Then a thought strikes me. I lean over the tailgate and drag my toolbox toward me. I open the metal box and grab a heavy wrench. As I smack it against my hand, Enrique nods approvingly.

"Got another one?"

I peer over the side panel into the box resting on the truck bed. "How about a hammer?"

"Hammer works."

I pass him the heavy claw-headed hammer and we edge through the trees to an overgrown footpath. When Ivy was seven or eight, I carried her up this very path after she sprained an ankle during a hike. It curves wide right and circles around to the side of the lodge. Going this way will take slightly longer, but it beats marching up the driveway fully exposed.

Do two grown men look silly sneaking up on a building in broad daylight while armed with tools? Yeah, I'm sure we do. But I'd rather be silly than dead. That's my motto. Enrique appears to share this view. His mouth is set in a firm line, and we don't speak as we approach the building on silent feet.

We press ourselves close to the side of the lodge and sidle around to the front. As we climb the stairs to the porch, I spot the busted-out window pane. Enrique has the keys ready when we reach the door, and he unlocks it with a quick, fluid movement and eases it open.

As soon as I set foot inside, I know the lodge is vacant. Dusty, still, quiet. But we walk through the empty lodge, scanning each room to ensure that it's empty. It is. Enrique's right, though. Someone *was* here. Two tracks cut parallel ribbons through the dust, left by the couch that was dragged from under the window to a nook near the fireplace.

"I'll bet they slept there." I point. "It's dark and has a clear view of both the front door and the kitchen."

He looks troubled. "Kids?"

"Maybe," I say. But it feels wrong.

After a beat, he gives his head a doubtful shake. "I don't know. Teenagers would be partying, not trying to get some shut-eye. And they sure wouldn't be worried about an ambush."

He has a point. I scan the room.

"Is anything missing?"

"Nothing obvious, at least not out here. I'll check the kitchen and the back office."

"See if you can find something to cover the window," I call after him.

"On it."

"Is there a broom around here?"

"Should be one in the janitor's closet." He jerks his thumb to the left before disappearing through the swinging doors to the kitchen.

I open the skinny door that he pointed out and peer inside. A mop and bucket, vacuum, and assorted cleaning supplies are crammed into the narrow closet, threatening to burst out at any moment. I grab the broom and dust pan and push the door closed before the rest of the equipment can spill out.

I sweep the glass into a pile and gather a warren of dust bunnies along the way. Enrique returns with a rectangular piece of cardboard and a roll of duct tape.

"Hang on," I tell him.

I step out onto the porch and use the broom handle to knock the remaining pieces of glass from the pane. They fall inside and hit the wood floor with a tinkle. Once the square is empty, I come back inside and sweep up the remaining shards.

He tosses me the tape, then positions the cardboard over the empty pane and holds it in place. I rip off a length of the silver tape and smooth it over one edge of the cardboard, then repeat the process three more times.

We both take a step back to examine our handiwork.

"It's better than nothing," I decree.

He nods. "I'll call the county when I get home. They're good about repairs. Should have it replaced in no time."

"Gonna call the cops, too?"

He grunts and rubs a hand over his scruff as he considers the question. Mistletoe Mountain doesn't maintain a police force of its own. When your town runs on a year-round supply of holiday goodwill and cheer, the boys in blue are somewhat superfluous. Technically, there *is* a police department, but it has a staff of zero. Dawn Min, our town manager, contracts with the county sheriff's office for any law enforcement services we might need. But calling in the sheriff is pricey and a sure way to land on Dawn's naughty list. She's a big proponent of working things out amongst ourselves—for free.

He grimaces. "Dunno. Hate to do it. But none of the food in the kitchen was disturbed. More evidence that it wasn't a bunch of kids."

"Probably," I agree. "Kids would have raided the snacks."

He meets my eyes. "So what then? It wasn't a burglary. Nothing's missing. Someone just needed a place to sleep?"

"Could be. Maybe they got kicked out of their house. Or they could be a runaway or a fugitive from the law. It could even be someone who crossed the border from Canada illegally." It's close enough to walk across, but illegal border crossings are virtually nonexistent here. In truth, none of these options seems likely, but I can't think of a better explanation.

After a beat, he sighs heavily. "I'll leave it up to the county parks office. If they want to report it, they can. It's their property."

I can't say I blame him for passing the buck. "We all done here, then?"

He walks through the quiet lodge, turning off lights, and checking locks while I empty the dustpan into the trash. I stow the broom and dustpan back in the closet, and we leave the same way we came in, locking the door behind us.

We hoof it down to my truck and toss the hammer and wrench back in my toolbox. I back out from the overhang of tree branches, kicking up a cloud of dust and gravel as I execute the tight turn from the trailhead to the unpaved road. As I drive, my mind's on the break-in. So when Enrique clears his throat, I expect him to advance another theory.

Instead he says, "You come up here for some quiet time before all the Christmas in July festivities start?"

I give him a sidelong glance.

"Shouldn't you be getting ready for the open house?" he presses.

"The girls are taking care of that."

I clock his frown in my peripheral vision. "You're not helping?"

"My sister's daughters came up from New Jersey," I tell him. "Between the six of them, they have it covered."

His frown deepens. "You and Carol, that was your biggest party of the year."

"It was," I agree. Emphasis on the past tense.

He falls silent, but not for long. "It's not true about Santa, is it?"

"Josh is playing Santa this year," I tell him. "Just needed a year off."

My words ring hollow, but I don't intend to elaborate. Enrique and I are friendly, not friends. We've had a few beers on the porch of my cabin, and a glass of bourbon every once in a while at his firepit. Sometimes we fish together. But we don't have the kind of relationship where I'm going to delve deep into my feelings about losing my wife.

When he speaks again, his voice is raspy and low. "You've got to take the time to grieve her. I know that. Just make sure you don't get stuck in it."

I slide my eyes toward him. "Sounds like you're speaking from experience."

He cracks his knuckles, one at a time, while he answers. "I am. My wife, Janessa, died in a car accident the year before I retired. Rainy night, slick roads. Some teenager lost control and T-boned her."

I grimace. "I'm sorry."

"It was rough not getting to say goodbye. But then I didn't have to watch her fade away gradually the way you did with Carol. Janessa was there, and then she wasn't. I'm not sure which way is better."

"It's always hard." I cringe at the platitude, but it's the best I can do.

He goes on. "The thing is, Nick, you reach an inflection point where grief turns you to stone. And if you aren't careful, you'll be cemented in that place for good. Believe me."

I don't know what to say to that, so I say nothing.

I slow the truck when we reach the edge of his property. As I come to a stop in the driveway, Bear appears in the cabin's front window, his giant front paws pressed against the glass. He barks a greeting.

As Enrique gets out of the truck, he says, "Thanks for your help. I hope I haven't overstepped, Nick. "

I lean over and call out the open passenger window, "You didn't overstep. I probably needed to hear it."

He turns back and gives me a short nod before jogging up the stairs to his porch. Bear's tail wags wildly, and I reverse out of the driveway.

CHAPTER 7

Noelle

I rush back to the library, practically bouncing. Farah's disappointment at the lack of cake is more than made up for by the excitement of the scavenger hunt.

"That's fire! What's the first clue?"

I hand her the small envelope and she scans the message. Even though I've already memorized it, I read it aloud over her shoulder: "Your first clue isn't difficult. The land of the sweets has many treats. Go to the place where you'll find a strong one."

"The land of the sweets?"

"Act II of *The Nutcracker*. All the different dances." I start ticking them off. I should know them by heart—from the ages of five through twelve, I danced in the Mistletoe Youth Ballet's annual performance, and have watched from the audience for even longer. "There's hot chocolate, marzipan, tea cakes …" Then it hits me, and I snap my fingers. "Arabian. The Arabian dance is coffee. Coffee can be strong."

"Unless you get it at the Snowflake Cafe," Farah says with a giggle.

It's true. Delphina's drink creations tend to be sweet concoctions, bordering on desserts. But I know for a fact she stocks a locally roasted Arabica bean blend to accommodate her best friend.

"Hmm. Maybe I'll stop over there after we close."

"Go now!"

"Farah, I've already left you alone for too long."

"Go now," she repeats, insistent. "You've been so sad and quiet lately. You need to do something fun."

I shoot her a sidelong look before I answer. It's true I've been more subdued than usual, but I don't love that she can tell I'm struggling.

"If you're sure."

She gives me a two-handed shove. "I'm positive."

"I won't be long," I promise. And then I'm running out of the library yet again.

I cross High Street, zip around the corner, and head down Silver Bell Lane to the Snowflake Cafe. The lunchtime rush has passed and the late afternoon regulars haven't yet shown up for their pick-me-ups. I push open the door, and the jingle bells overhead ring loudly in the empty cafe. Delphina's behind the counter, stocking a glass jar with cake pops that I recognize as Merry's handiwork.

"Hi, Ms. Winters."

Despite the fact that Delphina is an adult, a business

owner, and a member of my book club, she insists on calling me Ms. Winters. I get it. She's known me since she was reading board books on her mother's lap and wondering aloud if I lived at the library.

"Hey, Delphina. You really can call me Noelle," I remind her.

"Sorry. It's a habit," she says, sliding several chocolate reindeer pops in alongside the peppermint-candy-coated vanilla pops. "What can I get you, *Noelle?*"

I scan the chalked menu that hangs on the wall behind her. "I'll have a shakerato, please. A small one."

The absolute last thing I need right now is a caffeine kick. I'm already buzzing with excited energy, but I can't resist a good chilled shakerato on a hot afternoon. And Delphina happens to make one of the best I've ever had. It's borderline magical, taking me back to the sultry summer I spent in Ravenna—one of the few pleasant memories of that period of my life.

She pours a shot of espresso and leaves it to cool on the counter while she dumps a cup of ice and a few teaspoons of brown sugar into a cocktail shaker. Then she adds the espresso and shakes the tumbler vigorously for a full minute. While she strains the drink into a glass, I unfold the map and spread it out on the counter.

She hands me my beverage and leans over to take a look. "Cool map. Where'd you get it?"

I'm too busy savoring the sweet, airy crema that tops the drink to answer. "Mmm, heavenly."

"Thanks. The map?"

"I helped Holly and the gang bring the decorations down

from the attic. There was an envelope with my name on it tucked in with Carol's nutcrackers."

She grins at the mention of the nutcracker collection, then gives in to her curiosity. "What was in it?"

"This map and a note labeled Clue No. 1." I reach across the map and hand her the clue before she asks to see it.

She scans it and then looks up at me. "It's a reference to *The Nutcracker*, right?"

"Right."

"Okay. So the Sugar Plum Fairy has all the treats dance for Clara and the prince. Which one is strong?" She taps her lips in thought.

"The Arabian coffee dance," I tell her.

"Oh." Her eyes widen. "Oooh."

"You still get that Arabica blend for Holly, right?"

She nods. "Yeah. It's a little strong for my taste. I just used it in your espresso."

"Where do you order it from?"

"Stonebridge Roasters. All my beans are locally roasted. I just got a fresh delivery yesterday, " she tells me proudly.

"Was there a message or package for me?" I ask, feeling stupid.

"No, sorry. It was just a regular order. Twenty pounds of beans and an invoice." Then a thoughtful look crosses her face. "Stay right there!"

She disappears behind the swinging door into the back of the shop, and I sip my drink.

A moment later, she returns, clutching an envelope and wearing a triumphant expression. "Look!"

She hands me another tiny envelope. This one's labeled *Clue No. 2*.

"When did you get this?"

"I'd forgotten all about it. It was months ago—after last Christmas in July. But it was still hot. So August, maybe? Gray showed up with my delivery from Stonebridge Roasters. This envelope was taped to the invoice. I asked him about it, and he said he'd been asked to deliver it to me. He said at some point someone would come in asking for it and I should give it to them. I guess that's you."

"You didn't open it?" My tone oozes disbelief because there's no way I could have left an envelope labeled 'clue' sitting around unopened almost a year. My curiosity would drive me straight up the wall.

She shrugs. "I was busy. We were short-handed, so I tossed it in a drawer in the kitchen to deal with later. And then I forgot all about it."

"I don't suppose Gray told you who gave it to him?"

"I didn't ask. Like I said, I was busy. He was busy, too."

She watches as I carefully open the second envelope and scan the text. I read it aloud: *'Well done, you. Here's Clue Number 2. It's the seventh day of Christmas. What do you do?'*

We frown at each other over the paper.

"The seventh day of Christmas," she mutters.

We both start singing softly.

I get there first. "Seven swans a-swimming."

"Seven swans a-swimming," she repeats slowly.

The bell over the front door jangles loudly. I turn around to see who's come in, but nobody's there. The door swings back and forth. My eyes shift to the table in the corner where the local newspaper lies open, held down by a mismatched latte mug and saucer.

"Was someone in here when I came in? I didn't see anybody."

She jerks her chin toward the corner table. "There was a guy. He's probably in town for the festival. He ordered a peppermint latte and a snowball cookie, then camped out in the corner by the door with a copy of the *Mistletoe Press*."

I would have testified under oath that the coffeehouse was empty when I walked through the door. "How'd I miss him?"

"He wasn't very noticeable. He was really quiet. To be honest. I kind of forgot he was there." Her eyes widen. "He was wearing a hat and pair of big sunglasses. Maybe he didn't want to be noticed—or recognized. He could be famous, like an actor or a rock star avoiding the paparazzi."

I refrain from pointing out that Mistletoe Mountain has no paparazzi, and the rich and famous give us even wider berth. "Maybe."

I'm more interested in the newest clue than some almost certainly not famous random guy reading the weekly newspaper. "Seven swans a-swimming." I muse.

"Swans. Maybe they mean the Swansons."

I give her a look. I hope not. The Swansons live in a rambling red brick house at the edge of town. Vicky Swanson is one of my least favorite library patrons. She once asked me where the complaint box was. I directed her toward the suggestions box and she dedicated herself to stuffing it full of petty grievances until I relocated it to the recycling bin. I can't imagine the Swansons have the next clue. And if they do, I don't want it.

"Mr. Swanson's okay," she counters.

"I guess," I say without enthusiasm. "Let's come back to the Swansons. What else could it mean? Swimming could be a reference to the community pool. Maybe I'll head over there."

"Oh, not today," she says. "There's a swim meet with the team from the valley. The pool's closed to the public."

I drain my glass and slide it across the counter. "I should probably get back to the library anyway. Wherever the clue is, it'll still be there in the morning. Thanks for your help."

"Of course. It's fun."

I'm almost to the door when she calls after me. "Ms. Winters? I mean, Noelle?"

I turn back.

"How did Holly and her sisters seem this morning?"

I consider my answer. "They're doing okay. I think having the open house to focus on is good for them. It'll help them organize their memories of their mom around something happy. And I'm glad their cousins are there."

She hesitates, then says, "Mr. Jolly isn't helping?"

"No, he went up to the fishing cabin."

"He could use a friend to get him through this."

"He has loads of friends."

"Yeah, but you know what I mean. Not just a friend, someone who loved Mrs. Jolly as much as he did. Someone like you."

The words are a punch to my gut. I open my mouth to respond, but all that comes out is a whoosh of air.

"I'm sorry. I shouldn't have said that. You know how I am. As my mom likes to say, I don't believe in unexpressed thoughts."

I manage a gentle laugh. "It's okay, Delphina. I understand."

She's still shaking her head at herself, red-faced, when I step outside.

I take my time walking back to the library. The decorations are going up all along the square, glinting and glittering in the afternoon sun. The air crackles with excitement and anticipation as the festival weekend draws closer. In a few more days, the town will be packed with couples, families, and groups of friends basking in the summer holiday magic. I hate to think of Nick all alone in his cabin on the other side of Snow Lake.

The lake. Of course. The lake.

The lake is down the hill from the wine bar, where there's a cute covered deck so patrons can sit and sip their vino while they watch the white swans glide across the surface of the water. Several years ago, an eccentric resident willed the town a herd? No, flock? Lamentation. The word emerges from the depths of my overstuffed librarian brain. Mr. Johansen left a lamentation of downy white swans to the town when he passed away and they've been swanning around in Snow Lake ever since.

I don't know if there are seven of them, but I *am* sure that's where I'll find my next clue.

CHAPTER 8

Nick

I sit on the dock with a frosty mug of lemonade as I watch the swans glide across the surface of the lake. By the time I dropped off Enrique and got settled in the cabin, I'd missed lunch and my stomach let me know it. So I fried up some eggs and potatoes, ate, and cleaned the kitchen. At that point, I figured I might as well wait till tomorrow to fish.

The truth is, as everyone in the Jolly family well knows, I don't actually enjoy fishing. I hate the smell of the bait, recoil at the thought of putting it on the hook, and turn faintly green when I catch an actual fish. Don't even get me started on cleaning them.

What I love is the meditative part of it. The silence, the early morning chill, the sitting on the water and waiting. I suppose I could simply row out to the middle of the lake and float around in the boat for a while. And truth be told, on more than one occasion, I've not bothered to bait my hooks. Unsurprisingly, I caught nothing, and, equally unsurprisingly, those were some of my favorite 'fishing' expeditions.

Then there was the time I caught that line of silverbacks. Once, when I wasn't paying attention, Carol reached under the surface of the water and strung a six-pack of beer on my hook. When I felt the heavy tug, I started reeling it in. The girls, just little things then, jumped up and down on the bank, squealing and cheering. When I hoisted my catch—six cans of Frost Mountain Maple Ale—with a triumphant grin, Carol doubled over with laughter. I smile at the memory now even though it makes my chest hurt.

Fish or no fish, I need this reprieve from the bustle back at the inn as the girls and their cousins decorate, bake, and plan the events for the guests who'll start pouring in the day after tomorrow. Some of the returning visitors have stayed with us for ten, twelve, or more years. I'll go back to help with the actual open house on Friday. It would be unfair not to. But I want this time, this peace, to prepare for the gaiety, the joy, and the emptiness where Carol should be.

I kick off my trail shoes and plunge my feet into the cold water. Even on the hottest day in July, the glacial lake is bracing and invigorating. My splashing disturbs a nearby frog. He belches out a reproachful croak.

"Sorry, buddy."

He ribbits in response. I study the long grass near the bank until I spy him, hunkered down in the silty mud. Then my gaze drifts up the hill where I can just see the top of the ski lodge's stacked stone chimney. The break-in is stuck in the back of my mind, poking at me, prodding me. Like a piece of cornsilk wedged between my teeth or a pebble in my shoe.

My attention shifts to the rumble of a far-off car's engine. I squint across the lake as a cloud of dust rises up on the road that leads to the gazebo at the edge of the wine bar's property. I strain to make out the color or model of the car, but it's too far away. The car stops and the silhouetted figure of a woman wearing a long flowing skirt gets out and hurries to the covered deck. She squats and runs her hand along the underside of a bench.

Odd. And in light of the break-in at the lodge, suspicious. It's unlikely, but not impossible, that whatever this woman is up to is related to the break-in at the lodge. If, say, someone's using the lodge as a drug drop or other nefarious intent, they might also be passing messages at the gazebo. The tradeoff when a town, even a sleepy one, doesn't have a functional police force is that everyone's responsible for public safety. So I drain my glass and head back to the cabin to grab my binoculars. As I jog up the hill, it strikes me that I'm acting like the amateur sleuths in those books Noelle and my daughters consume like candy.

Still, I run into the cabin and grab the binoculars from the hook by the door. As I make my way down the driveway, I press the lenses to my eyes. But before I can focus on the woman, an unholy crashing reverberates in the woods to my right. I freeze, listening. If it's an animal, it's a big one. Maybe a moose or a deer. We don't see many bears here, but it could be a black bear. Or, I realize with a chill, it could be the most dangerous animal of all, the one that walks on two legs. But if it's a person stomping around in the woods, they're making no effort at stealth.

I drop the binoculars. They dangle from the strap, banging against my chest, as I creep toward the tree line following the sounds of someone or something thrashing through the woods. They're headed toward the lake. I tell myself that lots of people use these woods. There are hiking and mountain biking trails. And a wildflower meadow that leads to the waterfall is a popular picnicking spot. It could be anybody. This is undeniably true. But it doesn't stop me from plunging through the trees into the woods, the woman at the gazebo forgotten.

CHAPTER 9

Noelle

I debate waiting until morning to drive up to the lake to search for the second clue. But when I close up the library for the evening, there's still some daylight left. And, if I'm being honest, this scavenger hunt's the most fun I've had in months.

While some people might suggest dragging it out to savor it, I'm too excited for such restraint. Or, as Farah succinctly puts it, I have no chill. So as soon as I lock up the library, I race-walk back to my cottage on Poinsettia Way, slide behind the wheel of my little hatchback, and zip over to Santa's Cellar.

The sun hangs low over the purple mountains, its golden glow lighting the water like a flame, by the time I park near the lakeside gazebo. It's pretty and peaceful now. But once the sun dips behind the peaks, it'll get dark fast. And there are no lights on the road back to town. I didn't think to bring a flashlight, either. So I hurry across the gravel lot and search the undersides of the whitewashed benches for an envelope.

As I'm running my hand along the third of five benches, the circling swans out on the lake glide by, and I pause to watch their graceful choreography for a moment. I'm about to turn back to the task at hand, when a glint of light across the lake catches my eye.

The glimmer bobs along the path that leads from the Jollys' fishing cabin to the far side of the lake. There's a silhouette moving down the hillside from the cabin. The light is the setting sun bouncing off glass. If I have to guess, the glass is a set of binoculars pressed up against a face I can't quite make out. But I know it's Nick. I can tell by his gait, his shape.

I raise a hand in a halting greeting. Then, feeling self-conscious and exposed, I smooth it over my windswept hair as if that had been my intent all along. As I brush my hair out of my eyes, Nick's attention shifts and he jerks his head toward a loud noise in the woods. I hear it, too. Sound carries up here, echoing off the mountain behind the lake. I write off the sound as a group of mountain bikers or a family of deer. So I'm surprised when Nick veers off the path and runs into the woods.

The sun dips a little lower, and I remember why I'm out here. If I don't find the clue before the sun sets, I'm unlikely to find it until tomorrow. Putting Nick out of my mind, I resume my search of the gazebo. Nothing. Nada. Bupkus.

Frustrated, I fist my hands on my hips and think. While

this pagoda has the best view of the swans, there are other vantage points on the property—and off it. The swans are visible from the restaurant's outdoor seating area up the hill and from Nick and Noelle's dock. It's dinner time, so I don't want to traipse up to Santa's Cellar and start checking under the chairs, but I could drive around to the other side of the lake and check the Jollys' dock. And if I'm quick about it, I can look around and get off the property before Nick returns from the woods, avoiding an awkward conversation.

Mind made up, I hurry back to the car and follow the looping drive around the lake. I flick my gaze repeatedly to the woods to my left, searching for a glimpse of whoever's in the woods, but see nothing. I park near the lake and get out of the car, scanning the immediate area for a likely spot to hide an envelope. It has to be someplace protected from the elements and wildlife. There aren't too many options here. I eye the wooden platform that holds Merry's ten-frame beehive. The structure abuts a riotously blooming pollinator garden and would be a logical spot to hide the next clue, but there's a zero point zero percent chance, I'm sticking my hand anywhere near that thing. If I can't find the envelope without braving the hive, I'll ask Merry to check the next time she's up here gathering honey.

Giving the hive a wide berth, I continue along the path. There's a birdhouse and a squirrel feeder further up the hill. I'm willing to take my chances with non-stinging wildlife, so I shield my eyes from the glare of the fading sun on the water and head up the hill.

"*Noelle.*"

My name is a whisper on the wind. I whirl around,

expecting to see Nick. There's nobody there. I give a shaky laugh and try to write it off as a birdcall or a chittering squirrel. But the skin on the back of my neck is prickling and goosebumps rise on my arms. I stand rooted to the spot, listening hard.

There it is. A soft *crack,* as if someone has stepped on a twig. This is different from the noisy thwacking and thrashing I heard earlier. This is a stealthy sound. It sounds like someone is trying to sneak up behind me. My heart thumps and my mouth goes dry as I turn my head slightly and register motion at the periphery of my vision. A figure slips between the trees.

"Nick?" My voice is a rasp.

There's no answer, and I turn to stare into the woods. The branches of the tree closest to me sway slightly as if they've been brushed aside by movement. I jerk back. There's every chance I'm imagining things and spooking myself. But after Italy, I promised myself I would *always* honor my intuition. And right now, my intuition is screaming at me to run. *Run.*

But the trees are between me and my car, and I can't force myself to go past them. Instead, I lower my head and sprint toward the cabin on shaking legs. My throat burns and tears fill my eyes. I launch myself up the stairs to the front porch, where, for the second time in three days, I run smack into Nick Jolly's broad muscular chest.

CHAPTER 10

Nick

$\mathcal{I}$ trample through the brush, frustrated. There *was* someone out there, but they've vanished. Out of breath, I circle around to the cabin and mount the steps in the back. As I round the corner of the wraparound porch, I collide with someone and jerk back in surprise.

Instinctively, I plant my feet and raise my fists. My immediate thought is that whoever was in the woods is trying to get into my cabin. Before I can take a swing, my brain processes what I'm seeing and I exhale. It's Noelle.

She's shaking and panting, and I clasp her by her shoulders to steady her as I search her face and arms for injuries.

"Are you hurt?"

Her eyes are wide and her face is pale save for two bright red blotches on her cheeks.

"Nick, you startled me."

That makes two of us, I think. What I say is, "What's wrong?" Because clearly, something happened to terrify her.

She gives a shaky laugh. "I thought I heard someone."

"In the woods?"

She freezes. "Yes." Then she tries to brush it off. "Probably my imagination."

"There was someone in the woods," I tell her and immediately regret it.

Her chest heaves and her breath is shallow and too fast. She's hyperventilating.

I keep one hand on her arm while I unlock the door and ease it open. "Let's get you inside."

I guide her through the doorway and sit her down on the small couch by the hearth. She lets her head drop toward her knees. Once I'm sure she's steady on the seat, I hurry to the kitchen and pour a glass of water.

Crouching in front of her, I press the glass into her hands. "Drink."

She clutches it as she lifts her head. She gulps down some water before saying, "Thanks. I'm okay."

She's not, though. Her pulse flutters in her neck and sweat beads along her brow line.

"Why don't you tell me what happened?" I ease myself into the chair across from her.

She takes another sip before placing the glass carefully on a coaster, then wrings her hands. "I was across the lake—"

"At the gazebo?"

She nods. "Yeah."

"Why?"

"I was … looking for something."

I furrow my forehead at the vague response but let her continue.

"I thought it might be hidden by your dock. So I drove over here to check while you were in the woods." She takes a full breath and flutters her hands in the direction of the binoculars that are still hanging around my neck. "I watched you walk down the hill with your binoculars and then veer into the trees. I was walking up the path near the beehive, and I thought I heard someone whisper my name. I assumed it was you."

"It wasn't."

She nods. "I know. But when I turned around and you weren't there I *felt* someone watching me from the trees. I know how it sounds."

Unfortunately, it sounds believable. My chest tightens and I clench and release my fists in an effort to stay calm. "Where, exactly?"

"Behind the copse of quaking aspens near the edge of the wildflower garden."

I tighten my jaw. That's where I lost them—whoever they are. The fact that they were hidden in the woods spying on her fills me with rage and, I'll admit it, bone-deep fear.

"What were you looking for?" I ask.

A smile peeks through the worry on her face. "This is going to sound silly."

Great. I'll take silly over anxious any day—for both of us. I lean back in the chair and study her. "Hit me."

"I had tea at the inn today with your daughters and nieces."

"Elevenses. They told me before I left."

I split in a hurry this morning so I wouldn't run into her at the inn. As I fled my home for the cabin, I told myself it was because my brain and heart were too full of memories of all the times I walked into the kitchen to find my wife and her best friend doubled over with laughter while they had their late-morning tea.

"Right. After tea, I helped them bring the summer Christmas decorations down from the attic."

"I'm sure they appreciated it." What I'm not sure of is where this story is headed.

"I carried down the box with Carol's special nutcrackers."

My throat tightens. She loved those things—each one imbued with a story, a memory, an emotion.

Noelle continues, "I took them into the family room to set them up. When I opened the carton, I found an envelope addressed to me."

It takes me a minute to process this. "A letter from Carol?" I can't imagine what else it could be.

"That's what I thought at first, too. But the message is typed, and it's not signed. Then Holly told me that she and her sisters took down the family room decorations last year before you brought Carol from the hospital. The nutcrackers were already packed away when she came home. I don't see how she could have tucked it in that box unless she went up to the attic."

I nod. She's right. I hated to ask the girls to do it because I knew the familiar ornaments and decorations would have been comforting to Carol. But the only way to bring her home to die was to turn the parlor into an ad hoc hospital room. The tchotchkes had to go.

I realize she's waiting for a response. I push down the all-too familiar wave of grief, clear my throat, and cough out an answer with a short shake of my head. "There's no way she could have managed the stairs at that point. She was too weak."

We both fall silent for a long moment. Judging by her tight, drawn expression, she's remembering the last time she saw Carol. I watch as she pushes back a tsunami of emotion of her own.

She takes a breath before reaching into her pocket to pull out an envelope. "So the note, it wasn't a note so much as … well, here." She hands it over.

I unfold a small map and study it. It's not to scale, but the layout of the businesses in the town square looks about right. "It's a map of the town."

"Yeah, and the surrounding area."

"I've never seen this map before. It's not the one that the Chamber of Commerce hands out."

"I don't know where it came from either, but it's on my list of things to look into."

I point to two hand-drawn numbers. A one marks the inn, and a two designates the Snowflake Cafe. "Were these here?"

"No, I drew them. There was a note in the envelope marked Clue Number 1."

"A clue?" I echo.

"I think it's a scavenger hunt. I found the first clue at your inn, so I marked the spot with a one. The clue led me to the coffee shop where Delphina had another envelope."

"Clue Number 2?"

"Clue Number 2," she confirms.

"What did Delphina say about it?"

She blows out a long breath, ruffling the hair that frames her face. "She said it came in with an order of coffee beans at the end the summer last year. She was supposed to hold it until someone came in asking for it. She tossed it in a drawer and forgot about it until I showed up today."

"I don't understand."

"I don't either. Not really. But that second clue led me here."

"To my fishing cabin?"

"Well, to the lake." She fishes a small note card out of her skirt pocket and gestures for me to take it from her.

I scan it. "The seventh day of Christmas. Which one is that?"

"Seven swans a-swimming," she tells me.

"That's why you were at the gazebo overlooking the lake."

"Right. It's the best swan-watching spot I know of. But I didn't find another envelope. Then I thought, well, the first clue was at your home. Maybe the third clue is here."

I consider this. "You can't see the swans from in here."

"I know. That's why I was down at your dock. But I didn't see anything there." Her expression flattens. "Then I got spooked and took off. Anyway, maybe the clue isn't about the swans. It could be the community swimming pool." After a long pause, she says, "Like I said the whole thing is silly."

It is silly. But it's also the sort of game guaranteed to pique her interest. She loves puzzles, riddles, and mysteries. Whoever set this up knows her—and has access to my attic. I hand the clue back to her.

"Maybe the girls are behind this. I could see them thinking you'd have fun solving a little mystery."

Her eyes spark and she admits, "I am having fun with it. But your daughters seemed as surprised by the envelope as I was. Either they're better actors than I realize or they don't have anything to do with it. Honestly? I don't think I need to know who created it. It's harmless fun, right?"

It seems to be, but my brain snags on something that stops me from saying yes. "Probably," I allow.

"Anyway, thanks for the water. I should go. I'll come back and look for the clue in the morning when it's light out."

She starts to stand, and I place my hand on her arm to stop her as I realize what's nagging at me. "Don't."

"Why not?"

I hesitate. I don't want to frighten her, but I also don't want her tromping around near the woods alone. Not tonight, and not even in the light of day. "There was a break-in at the lodge."

Her green eyes go wide. "What?"

"Enrique flagged me down out on the road. Someone broke a window to get into the ski lodge. Doesn't look like they took anything, but between that and the fact that there *was* a person running through the woods, it's not a good idea. Stay here tonight, and we can look for your third clue together tomorrow."

Yes, I want her to stay because I'm not sure what's going on out in the woods and I want her to be safe. But it's more than that. I don't want to be alone. This realization sets me back on my metaphorical heels. My therapist is going to lose it when he hears this. Dane has been urging me to acknowledge what I want for months now. At first, right after Carol died, I was numb. Then after the heaviest grief eased a bit, I just felt flat. Colorless. Dane keeps probing me, pushing me to acknowledge that wanting Carol not to have died isn't a real answer. Well, this is. I want Noelle to stay. I'm not entirely sure how I feel about wanting this, but I can't deny that I want it.

She scrunches up her face. "Oh, Nick, I don't really think—"

"Please." My voice is gruffer than usual. "I'll make up the girls' bedroom for you. Then we can look for your clue together in the morning."

Her face goes still, and she studies me. After a pause that stretches out way too long, she says. "Sure, why not? I don't go into the library until the afternoon on Thursdays."

"Great. I'll get dinner started."

"Did you catch it?" Her smile is knowing.

What can I say, my fake fisherman status is an open secret around town. I lean into her amusement.

"That depends. By did I catch it, do you mean did I have the foresight to bring along a box of pasta and the fixings for a red sauce? If so, then, yep, I caught it."

When she's done giggling, I gesture for her to follow me into the kitchen.

Noelle

I dress baby salad greens and some tomatoes from Nick's garden in a balsamic vinaigrette then uncork a dusty bottle of chianti and leave it to breathe. I lean against the counter and watch him whip up a quick sauce while the pasta boils. The smell of garlic sizzling in olive oil fills the small kitchen and my stomach growls appreciatively. He tosses a handful of basil into the pan, followed by salt and pepper. Then he opens a can of crushed tomatoes and dumps them on top.

I hand him the red pepper flakes. "Homemade sauce. I'm impressed."

"Don't be. My Italian grandma would never pay for jarred sauce. She made hers the right way, simmered her Sunday gravy all day long. My sister still uses her recipe. This quick version can't compare, but it's better than the stuff in the supermarket."

He shakes the flakes into the sauce and gives it a stir. Watching him cook is disturbingly sexy. This thought pops unbidden into my brain. I give myself a horrified, silent scolding and distract myself from the way his rolled-up sleeves show off his tanned forearms by pouring the wine.

"Cin cin." The Italian toast emerges from the recesses of my mind.

I hand him a glass and he clinks it against mine. "Cheers. I forgot about your time in Italy. Don't judge my sauce too harshly, please."

I sip the smooth wine and smile. "Noted. Since I *do* use the grocery store stuff, you're safe."

The timer dings, and he jerks his chin. "Can you drain the pasta?"

I grab a potholder, carry the pot over to the colander he's set up in the sink, and dump the pasta. I give the colander a shake, return the pasta to the pot, and drizzle some olive oil on top. He nods approvingly and switches off the stove. We plate and sauce the pasta, wordlessly anticipating each other's movements in the cramped space. It's an oddly intimate silent dance and I'm hyperaware of his body in relation to mine as we work. His thigh grazes mine as he slides behind me to open the refrigerator, and heat surges to the surface of my skin. I freeze, not moving. Barely breathing, for that matter.

Maybe ease off the wine, I tell myself. Immediately ignoring myself, I take a big gulp.

He digs around in a kitchen drawer to find a cheese grater then shaves some fresh hard Parmesan on top of the pasta. I take my plate and the salad bowl and follow him to the tiny table. Once we're seated and have portioned out our salads, he gives me an unreadable look.

"What?"

"I almost said 'three things.'"

I furrow my brow. He says it like I should know what he's talking about, but I'm lost. "Three things?" I parrot.

He huffs out a quiet laugh and picks up his glass. "Sorry. Force of habit. When the girls were little, Carol started this nightly tradition at the dinner table. We'd go around the table and list three things from our day—one thing we were grateful for, one thing we regretted, and one thing we planned to do to make the next day a better day. We kept it up even after the girls moved out."

Three things sounds like a quintessentially Carol ritual. She was always finding ways to be present, be thankful, be *better*. I bite back the conflicting emotions stirred up and warring inside me—guilt, gratitude, uncertainty—and raise my glass.

"So, what's one thing you're grateful for?"

His voice is husky. "That's easy. I'm grateful that you agreed to stay. Sometimes, I think the loneliest part of my day is eating dinner by myself."

I blink at the raw honesty. "I can see that. I'm used to eating alone. To be honest, I like it. To me, there's nothing better than enjoying a good meal with a good book. But for years and years, you've had someone to talk to, to share those meals with."

"What are you grateful for?" he counters.

I don't have to think about it. "The scavenger hunt. I

haven't been feeling super festive lately. And that's hard when the entire town is in Christmas in July mode. But having an activity to focus on is lifting my spirits. Whoever planned this couldn't have timed it better."

I spear a tomato. After I chew and swallow, I say, "What's one thing you regret about your day?"

He pauses with a forkful of pasta halfway to his mouth and his expression tightens. "Not catching that bastard out there." He gestures at the outdoors through the floor-to-ceiling window.

Somehow, I forgot all about the watcher in the woods. Until now. I track the motion of his fork and turn to look out the window. The light has almost completely faded now. The lake glints silver in the distance. The trees gather in the shadows. Somewhere, a whip-poor-will chants his name. I shiver and look away fast. When I turn back to the table, he's watching me. His hazel eyes bore into me, like he's peering into my soul or something.

"What's your regret?"

I shovel some food into my mouth to buy time. He waits, patiently holding my gaze.

I exhale. "Regrets? I have a few. Not all from today, though."

"Any from today?"

I drink and think. "I regret wearing a skirt and sweater set," I answer lightly.

He cocks his head. "Why? It's a cute outfit. Very library lady."

"That's my vibe," I agree. "It's not really ideal for scavenger hunting, though. And definitely not my outfit of choice for an impromptu sleepover."

He dismisses the concern with a wave of his hand. "There's a drawer full of what the Jolly women call 'cabin clothes' in the bedroom. T-shirts, sweatpants, hoodies. You'll have your pick of comfies."

"Fuzzy socks to sleep in?" I can't sleep when my feet are cold. It's a thing.

"Almost certainly," he tells me in a mock-serious voice.

We finish our meal in companionable silence. Then we carry the dishes over to the sink. I wash, and he dries. And again, it feels like choreography. Like something we've been doing for ages. I consider whether maybe this is an old pattern from a million years ago, from London. And then I remember that I never once turned on the oven in my flat because I used it for sweater storage. No, the Nick and Noelle of the late nineties were anything but domestic.

I must giggle because he turns to me with a curious smile. "What's so funny?"

"Nothing. Just remembering my flat in London and its startling lack of closet space."

His grin widens. "I remember. You used your pantry as a linen closet and, if I'm not mistaken, your oven was your sweater drawer. That feels like a lifetime ago, doesn't it?"

"It does."

In part, I realize with a start, because we never talk about it. For more than two decades, when Nick, Carol, and I reminisced together, she and I told stories from our girlhood, he and she told stories about the early days of their relationship, and he and I told no stories. Shared no memories. Is that absence—the lack of shared history—what made Carol think I still had feelings for him?

He folds the dishtowel with a snap, drawing me out of my thoughts.

"Clean up's all done. Why don't we finish this bottle under the stars?" He picks up the chianti and the glasses and jerks his chin toward the back porch.

"Sure. I'll change into cabin clothes and meet you out there."

He opens the sliding glass door and steps outside, and I hurry down the hallway to the Jolly sisters' shared room. I feel around, patting the paneling on the wall just inside the door until my hand connects with the light switch. I flick it on and blink as my eyes adjust.

Two sets of bunk beds are pushed up against the side walls and a long low dresser anchors the far wall under the windows. I pull open the top drawer and dig out a pair of yoga pants that look like they might fit and a soft blue t-shirt that must be Holly's. It's emblazoned with the logo for her law school's 'Ambulance Chaser' 10K. I shed my librarian attire, step into the buttery pants, and yank the tee over my head. I let out an appreciative sigh as my comfort increases approximately ten thousand percent. I'd pay a small fortune to ditch my bra, too, but it feels inappropriate to go braless in this particular situation. So the girls remain captive in their underwire prison. Still, it's a vast improvement. I stack my discarded clothes in a neat pile and pad out to the hall, my bare feet slapping the floorboards.

❄

I SLIDE the kitchen door open and join Nick at the cedar table built into one corner of the porch. The exterior lights are off, but the glow from the light over the kitchen sink spills out in a diffuse halo. He pushes my glass toward me. I settle onto the bench beside him and inhale deeply. The warm air carries the sweet scent of wildflowers and the soft chanting of the birds. Fireflies twinkle in the meadow behind the house.

"Comfy?"

"Mmm-hmm." I take a contented sip of my drink.

"Look up," he suggests, tipping his head back.

I do the same. The sky is already a dark purple. A silver sliver of a crescent moon hangs over the shadow of the mountains. And the stars. The sky is an explosion of bright pinpricks. There's not much light pollution in town, but this display is next level.

Awe flows through me, filling my chest. "Wow," I breathe.

"This is my favorite thing about the cabin."

"I can see why."

We sit side by side, our throats open to the sky and soak in the celestial display. His shoulder is pressed up against my bare arm and an image flashes in my mind. We're sitting in Regent's Park in London, a picnic blanket spread out on the ground, Nick's arm draped over my shoulder as I snuggle into his side, staring out at another panoramic view.

"This reminds me of watching the sunset from Primrose Hill," he says in a low voice.

A shiver runs along my spine. "I was just remembering that night."

I feel his gaze slide away from the stars and toward me. "Yeah?"

"Yeah."

I leave unsaid the rest of that memory. I wonder if it's playing out in his mind, too. That night, when I met him after he got off work and we had a sunset picnic in a spot famous for its romantic vibe ended exactly how we both knew it would.

I wriggle slightly so we're no longer touching and reach for the wine bottle. I top off my glass, and then his. He raises the glass toward me then takes a sip without moving his eyes away from my face. Based on the heat in his gaze, he's also thinking about the first time we slept together.

Is his face moving closer to mine? Yes, he's definitely leaning toward me. My pulse flutters. Why am I thinking about his mouth covering mine, the pressure of his lips, the salty taste of his tongue?

I gulp my wine and blurt, "So, what's the third thing?"

He freezes. "What?"

"The third thing. What is it—something to do better tomorrow?"

The intensity in his eyes fades, and he pulls back. "Oh. Yeah. What's one thing you're going to do to make tomorrow a brighter day?"

The moment successfully interrupted, I relax, too. "I'm going to let you join my scavenger hunt so you don't have to pretend to fish."

He laughs. "Very charitable."

"And what will you do to make tomorrow a brighter day?"

"What am I going to do?" He takes a drink while he considers the question. Then he snaps his fingers. "Got it."

I raise my eyebrows in a question.

"I'm gonna raid Merry's herb garden out back and make my famous herb frittata for breakfast."

Relieved at being on less fraught footing, I give him a skeptical look. "It's famous, huh?"

"Maybe not internationally famous. Locally famous."

I purse my lips. "I'm a good judge of frittatas, you know. Hope you can back up this claim."

"Oh, I can. It'll be a match for anything you've tried in the past."

Our easy banter pushes the earlier weirdness out of my mind. "Talk to me about these herbs."

"Some chives, a little dill, sage, parsley. But the secret ingredient is fennel."

"Hmm. That sounds like an authentic frittata. Italians love their fennel in almost everything." I laugh at a memory. "My landlady in Ravenna served sliced raw fennel at the end of every meal. She called it a palate cleanser."

"You know, I always wondered what happened in Italy."

His tone is casual, but the question sets my teeth on edge.

"What do you mean, what happened?"

"The last I heard, you had that traineeship at Oxford and then a research position for the summer at the University of Bologna. When Carol tracked you down you were about to start the masters' program in Italy. Then you came back to Mistletoe Mountain for our wedding and never left."

"Oh—I don't know. I guess I missed home," I say lamely.

I feel the weight of his gaze as he studies me by the starlight.

"Don't BS me, Noelle. What happened?"

Panic rises in my chest. "Nothing. It just wasn't a good

situation. I wasn't really looking forward to going back, to be honest. Then, if you remember, Vashti's daughter had her triplets two months early, and Vashti resigned to move to Illinois to help take care of her grandbabies. Suddenly, the Mistletoe library needed a director on short notice. And there I was. A job that I never thought would open up fell into my lap. It was serendipity."

"Do you ever regret it? Staying here?"

I tilt my head and give him a curious look. "No. Does it seem like I do?"

He shrugs and swirls the liquid in his glass. "I don't know. The Noelle I met in London was chock-full of dreams, big ones. Don't get me wrong, Mistletoe Mountain's a special place. I know that better than most, but it's not a big place. Don't you ever feel constricted?"

"No," I tell him honestly. "I can do whatever I want at the library. I don't have to deal with bureaucracy or hierarchy. I can make a difference in this community. Besides, little places can accommodate big dreams. I love this big little place."

He squints at me as if he's not entirely convinced. "And you don't feel like you've missed out? I don't mean professionally. Personally."

"I'm not lonely." I sip my wine, and then amend my defensive answer. "That's not entirely true. Sometimes I'm lonely. Sometimes I look around and wonder how I ended up in my forties, without a partner or a family. But, on balance, I'm happy and fulfilled."

"Why don't you date more?" he asks.

I snort. "Have you looked around? Josh Morgenthal's taken."

"Come on. I'm being serious."

"So am I. Pretty much everyone in this town is coupled up, unless I'm looking for a guy in his early twenties. And I'm not the cougar type."

He considers this. "I guess the local dating pool is kind of shallow. I never really thought about it."

"You haven't had to." *Yet.*

I wonder, will he start dating? Nick Jolly, eligible widower? Carol certainly didn't want him to live his days out alone.

As if he's reading my mind, he says, "I can't imagine ever putting myself back out on the dating scene."

"No?"

"No." He turns to look directly at me again, and, yet again, his eyes are molten. "What are the odds I'll find a true partner? I'm not sure lightning will strike a third time."

I clear my throat. "You mean second."

"No, Noe. I mean third."

I hold his gaze. Unbidden, my tongue darts out and wets my lips. He follows the motion, and his Adam's apple bobs. The air between us crackles. My heart thumps against my breastbone.

He's a magnet, pulling me toward him. I see myself leaning in, digging my fingers into his thick hair, and … I jump up from the bench before I can do something irreversible.

"Good night, Nick," I croak. Then I run into the cabin.

CHAPTER 12

Nick

I sit, stunned, as Noelle flees the porch for the safety of the guest room. I almost *kissed* her. Twice, actually. What the hell am I doing? I haven't felt a sliver of sexual attraction or interest in the eleven months since Carol died. Until now. Now, the evidence is undeniable. I polish off the wine and wait for my heart rate to return to normal before I go inside and dick around in the kitchen, wiping down already clean counters and setting up the coffeemaker to brew in the morning.

Out of tasks, but still too amped up to sleep, I pad out to the living room to listen to music. When we bought the cabin, the previous owners left behind an old vinyl record player. At first, Carol and I viewed it mostly as a curiosity. Turns out, though, there's something meditative about the ritual of putting on a pair of over-the-ear headphones and tethering myself to the player physically. It's immersive. I don't scroll my phone. I'm not distracted. I can connect to the music in a way that I don't when I'm streaming something on my playlist. I could use to focus on something other than Noelle's rosebud lips right about now.

I flip through the handful of albums picked up at garage sales and used record stores over the years. It's a slim, eclectic collection based mainly on availability, with one exception. I slip it from its sleeve, a record by blues legend Buddy Guy, lift the record player's lid, and gently ease the disc onto the turntable. I put the arm down, settle the headphones over my ears, and sit back in my chair, my legs stretched out in front of me. Then I tip my head back, closing my eyes and letting the mournful melody wash over me.

Memories of the time Carol and I went to see Buddy play in Chicago surge to mind. It was our tenth anniversary, a rare trip without our girls. The song changes, and I'm watching the sun set over London with Noelle tucked into my side while James Taylor croons from a nearby boombox. Carol. Noelle. Carol. Noelle. Their faces flip back and forth in my mind as memories from London and memories from my decades of marriage swirl together. I scrub my hands over my face and groan.

Guilt bubbles up. I almost kissed her. If she hadn't pulled back, I wouldn't have stopped, and I don't know what to make of that. Would that have been a betrayal? But in the next instant, I imagine Carol rolling her eyes at that notion. She never asked about my relationship with Noelle, never acted intimidated or threatened when Noelle moved back to town. She was delighted to have her friend back in her life. My wife didn't have jealousy as a personality trait. She was confident in the fact that I loved her. She was right to be confident, because I did—I loved Carol completely and utterly. And I'll always love her.

And Noelle Winters was my first love. She may be ancient history. But she's still in my bones, in my blood. That's not a betrayal, it's an artifact. Still, I lean forward and turn the music up in a fruitless attempt to drive out the image of Noelle staring up at me, her green eyes sparking in the dark, her pulse fluttering in her throat. It felt right to want to kiss her. It felt inevitable.

The A side of the album ends, and I'm tired enough to turn it off rather than flip it over. I go to the hall bathroom to brush my teeth and splash some water on my face. On my way past Noelle's room, I notice the light coming from under the door and pause. I could knock and make sure she has blankets and pillows. But the air in the cabin is still charged, electrified, and I don't trust myself.

I force myself to walk past her door to my room and then I lay awake, my heart racing, acutely aware that she's just feet away on the other side of the thin wall. And I'm transported across an ocean, through the decades, to another room with thin walls. A stuffy, unair-conditioned flat on a sultry summer night. Noelle's head is thrown back and her throat exposed— she's vulnerable, open, trusting. I groan and flop onto my side. I need to get her out of my mind.

"Hotels."

It's an old trick, better than counting sheep. I pick a category and run through the alphabet, naming hotels and resorts for each letter until I quiet my thoughts. I make it all the way to the Regency before my eyelids grow heavy and my breathing slows. Now I just need to make it through the night without dreaming about her.

CHAPTER 13

Noelle
Thursday

 wake to the soft sunlight slanting through the blinds, the chirping of songbirds, and the glorious, unmistakable smell of coffee brewing. After a quick trip to the bathroom to run my fingers through my hair and brush my teeth with the toothbrush I found in a package under the sink, I pull the borrowed hoodie over my head and follow my nose to the kitchen and the source of caffeine.

"Morning, sunshine," Nick says casually.

He leans against the counter with a red, hand-thrown 'Mr. Claus' mug to his lips and a pair of loose sweatpants hanging low on his hips. He places his coffee on the counter and reaches behind him to pull the coordinating green 'Mrs. Claus' mug down from the hook over the sink. As he stretches, his t-shirt rides up to reveal taut, tanned abs. I manage to pull my gaze away from the display before he catches me looking.

He fills the mug with coffee and presses it into my eager hands.

I inhale the aromatic steam and sigh a deeply contented sigh. "Ah, thanks."

"Did you sleep okay?"

Sure, except for all the sex dreams. Leaving *that* thought unexpressed, I chirp, "Like a log."

"Good, then you should have plenty of energy for this morning's activity."

My brain zings back to my dreams, and my face warms. "What activity is that?" I squeak.

He gives me a curious look. "The scavenger hunt."

I drag my mind out of the gutter. "Right. The scavenger hunt. I guess we should check the outdoor setting area at the restaurant. That has a partial view of the lake."

He bobs his head. "Maybe. Come help me cut the herbs for the frittata, and I'll tell you what I was thinking."

He grabs a basket and a pair of shears from a shelf near the door, and I trail him out to the porch, cupping my hands around the oversized mug. The early morning air is cool but the promise of heat shimmers just under the surface. *Just like us.* I really, really need to stop having these thoughts.

He leads the way to a raised box herb garden that I'm sure was laid out to be tidy but is now riotous and in full July bloom. Fragrant mint spills over the edges and purple lavender sways in the breeze. He hands me the basket, and I place my coffee mug on the retaining wall. We both crouch in the garden. He snips some chives, dill, sage, and parsley and drops the herbs into the basket.

"Before we go to Santa's Cellar, there's another spot we should check first. It has a perfect view of the swans." He grins up at me and a shock of hair falls over his eyes. He pushes it away with the back of his hand and the skin around his eyes crinkles in the sunlight.

"Really?"

"You know the waterfall?"

"Sure."

"Back behind it, there's a rock outcropping with a big, flat rock. Lots of people use it as a picnic spot."

I search my memory. "I remember. I mean, I haven't been up there in years and years. But when I was a girl, I used to play up there." Then I frown. "It doesn't have a view of the lake, though."

"Probably not back then," he agrees. "But before they opened the wine bar, the owners had to clear some trees to get their equipment in. They took down a copse of invasive buckthorn trees. After the work was done, they planted blueberry bushes. So now there's a perfect view of just a slice of the lake. I know for a fact that you can see the swans from there."

Any worry I had that today would be awkward slips away as the thrill of the hunt overtakes me. We head back inside, and I help Nick prepare breakfast—not that he needs my help. It's clear that, over the quarter century of running the inn, he's developed culinary skills that far outpace mine. I've been known to call a spoonful of peanut butter scooped from the jar a perfectly reasonable breakfast. So, this savory homemade deliciousness leaves me swooning.

We make quick work of cleaning the kitchen, and he fills two stainless steel canteens with water while I dig around in his daughters' shared closet for a pair of hiking boots that fit. We're out the door before the day heats up.

The hike up to the waterfall is rocky, but the rise is gradual. A third of the way up, I feel eyes on my back and freeze. Nick's a half-step ahead of me.

"Nick," I whisper-hiss his name. "There's someone in the bushes."

He turns slowly and scans the vegetation. Then a smile breaks across his mouth, and he gestures for me to step up to join him. When I do, he points to the left. "Look."

A white-tailed doe peers out at us from the leaves, her wide eyes unblinking. Two fawns stand behind her like a pair of statues.

"Oh," I breathe.

The mama deer watches us with caution as we continue on our way up the hill. Around the bend, the rush of water over rocks announces that we've nearly reached the waterfall. We move on, winding past and above the white falls until we come to the outcropping.

He turns back to me. "You go first. I'll spot you."

I'm a decent hiker, but I have a mild fear of heights. I wonder if he remembers.

A moment later, he removes all doubt. "Just in case you get dizzy like you did when we were on the terrace at the top of the Arc de Triomphe."

Yeah, he remembers. Although in fairness, my vertigo all

those years in Paris was probably due in equal parts to the surveying the city from a height of fifty meters and my heightened emotion at the realization that when the weekend was over, so was our whirlwind romance. I remember staring out at the lights and being overcome with sadness.

Now, I shake my head, dislodging the memory, and muster up a smile. "It's not that high, but thanks."

As I sidle by, my arm brushes against his. A frisson of electricity jolts through me at the contact. I hurry past him, take a deep breath, and gain a foothold in the rocks.

We scrabble up the rock face without any drama—except for the internal drama caused by the fact that I'm acutely aware of Nick two feet behind me with a perfect view of my butt. I take a moment to silently thank Griselda for her obsession with lunges and squats in her Booty Boot Camp. I may have cursed her at the time, but I'm grateful now. And not just because it makes the hike easier.

I reach the top of the outcropping and hoist myself up onto the flat rock in an inelegant, but effective, floppy fish motion. I settle myself on the surface, shrug out of the light daypack Nick lent me, and reach for my water bottle while he pulls himself up beside me. I pretend not to notice his lat muscles straining against the back of his thin tee-shirt as he boosts himself onto the rock in an explosion of power.

"Show off," I pant, sucking down water.

He snickers. "I owe it all to Grizzy's Lumber-Jacked program. Well, that and chopping wood for the inn. Functional fitness for the win." He twists off his canteen's cap and guzzles a long swig of water. Then he gestures to the vista of the valley below. "As promised, there's the lake."

I nod. Far below, Snow Lake shimmers in the sun. Several white swans glide gracefully over the water's surface. Then I scan the mountaintop. "This could be the spot. But where would someone hide a note here?"

He twists his mouth to the side and narrows his eyes as he surveys our surroundings, too. "It has to be somewhere protected from the elements."

"And where someone won't stumble across it accidentally."

"Hmm." He stands and makes a slow turn.

Disappointment threatens to crowd out my triumph at reaching the summit. Did we make this climb for no reason? I hold out my hand, and he pulls me to my feet. I stand beside him and take a careful look around.

"Where would I hide an envelope up here?" I wonder aloud.

He shakes his head. "I guess we can start turning over rocks."

"Yikes, no. I'm looking for a clue not a nest of timber rattlers."

"Fair point."

We stand in stymied silence staring at the rocky ground for a long moment. Then I walk to the edge of the rock and look down. The landscape dissolves into a fuzzy, long-ago memory and I whip my head around and ask, "Is there an easy way down to the blueberry bushes?"

"Sure. It's a steep footpath, but it's well-worn. You need a snack?"

"I wouldn't turn down fresh blueberries. But no, I just remembered something." My words tumble out in a rush.

"Back when dinosaurs roamed the earth, Mistletoe Mountain had an Elf Troop."

"A what now?"

"It was a coed scouting program. It disbanded at some point. But when I was in elementary and middle school, *everyone* was in the Elf Troop. And for a few years in the late eighties, letterboxing was all the rage. I know there was a letterbox under the buckthorns. I remember stamping my log there."

He gives me a blank look. "Letterboxing?"

I grin at the memory. "An outdoor treasure hunt. Think geocaching, but analog. A lot of the clues were word of mouth, and some of them were in the *Mistletoe Missive*. We'd search for these weatherproof boxes. When you found one, you wanted to remove it in secret so you wouldn't ruin the game for anyone else. Inside, there was an ink pad and a stamp to add to your personal logbook, along with a logbook that you would stamp with your stamp. Then you put everything back and hid the box again."

"Letterboxing, huh? Never heard of it. And everyone in town did this?"

"Everyone," I confirmed. "And I specifically remember that Carol, Rudy, and I found the letterbox buried under the buckthorn trees together. We were the third group to stamp the log." I nod toward the blueberry bushes.

"Huh. You know if the box was still there when the trees were dug up, it might have been destroyed or removed."

"Sure. But there's only one way to find out."

We each take another drink of cool water before closing up our bottles and shouldering our packs. We step off the ledge and edge our way down the steep hill, sliding through loose soil and gravel as we descend. Nick's in the lead, which turns out to be both good and bad.

It's good, because when I get too much momentum and slam into his back, hard, he breaks my fall. And it's bad, because when I crash into him, I send both of us tumbling into the tangle of blueberry bushes.

"Oof." He lands on his stomach with his head under a bush and me sprawled out over his back in a superman position.

I yelp and scrabble off him. I roll onto my back in the dirt beside him, breathing heavily.

"Sorry," I whimper when I have enough air in my lungs to speak.

Next to me, his broad shoulders shake.

"Are you okay?" I pop up and prop myself onto one elbow, worried that I hurt him. Then he flops over on his back and I can see that he's shaking with silent laughter. I smack him lightly on the chest. "You scared me!"

He grabs my wrist and holds it flat against his beating heart. "I'm just glad blueberry bushes don't have thorns."

Now we're both laughing, big whooping laughs, as we imagine getting a face full of thorns. His eyes soften, and I realize he's stroking the underside of my wrist. My throat tightens and my laughter dies. I disengage my hand and sit up.

"Come on. Let's look for the box."

He cocks his head and gives me a searching look that I pretend not to notice as I push aside the nearest bunch of branches and peer into the bushes. He squats beside me and swims his arms through the next bush. We spot the green plastic container nestled at the base of his bush at the same time. We both reach for it.

He pulls back his hand. "You do the honors."

"Thanks." I grab the strap and drag the waterproof box through the bushes.

He leans in to examine the container. "Is that a decon container?"

I nod. "Yeah, the troop bought a bunch of them from the army surplus store. They're perfect letterboxing boxes."

I remove the lid and shake out an age-yellowed logbook, a dried-up red ink pad, a rubber stamp in the shape of a snowflake, and a linen envelope labeled *Clue No. 3.*

CHAPTER 14

Nick

The third clue sends us into town. We return all the other stuff to the army green plastic container, even though I sincerely doubt kids still letterbox, then haul our butts back down the mountain. I may or may not let Noelle go ahead of me so I can enjoy the view of the butt she's hauling during the journey to the fishing cabin. We agree to take her car into town. Since I'm supposed to be hiding out at the cabin, I don't exactly want my pickup truck to be spotted.

As she drives, I re-read the clue: *This clue's got a twist. But don't you think she gets the better end of the deal? After all, her hair will grow back. His pocket watch is gone forever.*

"O. Henry, right?"

She nods. "Right, 'The Gift of the Magi.' It's gotta be."

"Are you thinking the library? Or the maybe the bookstore?"

She taps a finger against her lip, thinking. "Maybe, if the clue is the book itself. But the clue focuses on the gifts the couple exchanged. So it could be the hair salon or the barber shop."

"Or Alpine Jewelers," I suggest.

She twists in her seat and flashes me a bright smile. "You're a genius! I'll bet it is the jewelry store. It seems like Xander carries one of everything in that place."

Both sides of High Street are completely parked up—not surprising, given that the festival's official opening is tomorrow. Our little town is filling up. Noelle bypasses the paid parking garage and zips down the alley to the lot behind the library. We leave her car in the reserved director's spot, which I'm frankly surprised is open. Everyone in town knows she rarely uses the perk. Her cottage is just a short walk from the library, so I figured we'd find some time-pressed patron illegally parked in the spot. But apparently, Mistletoe Mountain had a soft spot for its feisty, friendly library director.

By unspoken agreement, we hoof it down the cobblestone alley instead of maneuvering through the pedestrian traffic on High Street. When we reach the courtyard behind the pair of historic townhouses that are home to Alpine Jewelers and the North Pole Social Club, she lifts the latch on the wrought-iron gate. We cross the yard, slip through the narrow passage on the side of the building, and dodge the flow of foot traffic to enter the shop.

The little jewelry store is bustling, so we kill some time checking out the displays while Xander Michaelson, whose family has owned the shop since the beginning of time, helps a giggly young couple looking at rings and then waits on a man who's picking up his repaired watch. Finally, it's just us and, and he turns to us.

"Nick, Noelle, what can I do for you folks?"

"It's your party," I tell Noelle under my breath. "You take the lead."

She steps forward. "Hi, Xander. This might sound like an odd request, but do you have a platinum pocket watch chain and a set of jeweled hair combs?"

His eyes twinkle behind his wire-rimmed glasses. "Are the Mountainside Players doing a reading of 'The Gift of the Magi' this weekend?"

"No. But you're on the right track." She turns to me. "Show him the note."

I hand over the little envelope as requested, and she continues, "Nick and I are doing a scavenger hunt, and this was our last clue."

He scans the note, and a slow smile spreads over his face. "I wondered when someone would be in for this. I don't always have pocket watch chains or ornate hair combs in stock. But I do keep a display set in the window. They're not for sale. Just a fun nod to the story."

He gestures toward the front display case. Somehow in the twenty minutes we spent cooling our heels, neither of us noticed it.

"And you've been expecting someone to ask about it?"

Noelle's voice is warm and friendly. But her tapping foot gives her away, at least to me. Xander is a methodical, serenely unhurried individual who devotes his full attention to each customer, each task, and each conversation with the focus of a Zen master. Neither speed nor succinct answers is his strength.

"Oh, yes." He pauses to think. Her toe taps faster. "Hmm, it must have been right around this time. No, wait. That's not right. It was just *after* Christmas in July. Perhaps early August? Definitely before the fall festivities began. I could check my diary and see if I made a note of the precise date."

"No need," I assure him, giving Noelle a cautious look.

For all his tranquility, Xander lacks an instinct for self-preservation. If he doesn't hurry this story along, Noelle's going to shake it out of him.

He continues, "One morning, I unlocked the door to find that someone had slipped a note through the mail slot."

"A note," she repeats, her face flushing with excitement.

I used to know how to bring that color into her face. The stray thought comes out of nowhere. I shove it back into its box and try to focus on the conversation.

"Yes, a note and a small ivory envelope labeled *Clue No. 4.* The note asked me to hold the clue until someone came in asking about the pocket watch and combs. So I tucked it under the display for safekeeping."

He strolls to the window in slow motion with Noelle tripping on his heels. I trail behind. He takes a small key from his pocket, unlocks the window, and freezes.

"Something wrong?" I ask.

He twists his neck to look at me with a confused expression. "This glass is smeared."

I peer over his shoulder. He's right. There's a big, greasy

handprint on the glass. "Someone probably rested a sweaty hand there while they were checking out the display."

He flattens his lips at the suggestion. "That's highly unlikely. I personally clean this glass several times a day. I'm particular about it." He gives a small shrug of acknowledgment, as if he realizes he's fastidious, before he continues. "Aside from that, this is a window case. The display faces the street; there's nothing to see from this side."

"Hmm. That's so weird," Noelle murmurs sympathetically, giving me a wide-eyed look behind his back.

"It truly is." Finally, he slides his hand under a stand that holds the pocket watch and hair combs, retrieves a small envelope, and holds it out to her.

She snatches it from his hand. "Thank you."

"It's my pleasure." Then he turns to me. "Nick, I was sorry to hear you're not going to be our Santa this weekend."

I suppress a sigh. "I don't have a lot of cheer this year. It wouldn't be fair to the kids to have a sad Santa."

He nods, thoughtful and understanding. "I mean no disrespect to Josh. He'll do a great job, but I sure wish you'd reconsider. It won't be the same without you. You're an institution around here. You *are* Summer Santa."

I never realized I was an institution, but Enzo said the same thing. It makes me feel old. I vaguely mumble something about getting back in the Santa saddle next year and am saved from further conversation when the bell over his front door jingles and a clutch of women wearing red sequined Santa hats sweeps into the store in a cloud of perfume and chatter. We thank Xander and seize the opportunity to make our escape.

Noelle beelines for the courtyard behind the shop and plops down on an ornate iron bench. "Ready to open it?"

"Let's do it." I drop down next to her.

Just as she's about to slit the envelope open, my phone chirps in my pocket. She pauses while I pull it out and check the display.

"It's Ivy. Give me a minute?"

"Of course."

I pick up the call. "Hi, honey. Everything okay?"

"Yeah, Dad, things are great here. The cousins have been a *huge* help. And they're a lot of fun, too."

"Glad to hear it."

"We're pretty much all set for the open house. Merry and Rosemary are cooking up a storm. Holly made a color-coded, timed checklist of everything we need to do." She snorts at her oldest sister's intensity before continuing. "Thyme put all the decorations up and I got the guest rooms ready while Sage set up special crafts for the kids. We have games. We have music. And we're all set for the first check-ins this afternoon."

"Sounds like you're kicking butt and taking names."

"Yeah, we are. I'm not just calling with an update, though. I'm sorry to bother you at the cabin, but I thought you should know."

I don't bother to correct her as to my whereabouts. "Know what?"

"Jamal just stopped by. He wanted to let you know that Mr. Morgenthal won't be able to play Santa this weekend after all."

"Why? Did something happen to Josh?"

Noelle looks up with concern at the question.

On the phone, Ivy hurries to reassure me. "He's fine. But Ryan's mother fell and broke her elbow and her knee. She's going to be okay, but she lives alone, so she needs some help. Ryan's flying out to California to give her a hand, and Josh doesn't want him to have to go alone. They're not sure how long they're going to be. At least a week, probably longer. Jamal said Josh would've tracked you down himself but they're already on their way to the airport. He's really sorry, though."

"He shouldn't be. Family comes first. Thanks for letting me know."

"Jamal said to let him know if you want him to find another replacement. He can't sub in himself because he's running the reindeer relays."

I pause, but only for a beat. Xander was right. I am Summer Santa. Pushing it off on Josh never felt completely right, and now that the job's back in my lap, I need to step up and suit up in the summer-weight Santa suit.

"No, I'll do it. I just need to track down the suit." I hear squealing and shouting in the background. "Am I on speaker?"

"Oh, uh, yeah. We were hoping that's what you say," Ivy confesses.

"No worries, Dad. Jamal brought your suit. It's hanging in the hall closet," Holly shouts.

"Love you, Santa!" Merry says.

"About the suit, Dad. Josh may have had it altered," Ivy explains.

"Understood. I'll see you soon," I tell my celebrating daughters. Then, shaking my head, I end the call and catch Noelle's eyes. "Did you get all that?"

"The gist. Ryan's mom needs some help?"

"Yeah. She broke her elbow and her knee."

"I'm sorry she got hurt, but senior roller derby is no joke."

"Ryan's mother is on a roller derby team? Isn't she, like, a hundred?"

"At least. But I'm told she's one heck of a jammer." A soft smile touches her lips. "I'm glad you're going to be Santa."

I'm not entirely sure how I feel about it, but I return the smile. Then I gesture toward the envelope. "Can we put this clue on hold for a few hours? I need to make sure the suit still fits. If Josh already had it taken in, I'm going to need to do some emergency alterations."

My imagination must be playing tricks on me because it looks exactly as if she's running her eyes over my chest and shoulders with a greedy expression. "Right, of course." She checks her watch. "Why don't you stop by the library after you get your costume sorted out and we'll open the clue then?"

"It's a date—I mean, a plan. Not a date. It's a *plan*." I trip over my words like a schoolboy, but she just gives me a puzzled look. Get a grip, Jolly.

CHAPTER 15

Noelle

After I send Farah off with instructions to spread the news that Nick Jolly *will* be appearing as Santa Claus this weekend, I settle behind the circulation desk and flip through the morning's messages. I have a private office—a nice one—but I'd rather be out here on the floor with my community, so I rarely use the director's space. I can't wipe the grin off my face at the thought of Nick putting on the Santa suit. Judging by the excited conversation and laughter of the library patrons, I'm not the only one. I hate that Ryan's mom's been injured, but if it had to happen, she picked a good time. And Lois is a tough bird. She'll bounce back.

I open the grant proposal instruction packet I've been avoiding all week. But the dry, technical language is no match for the distraction in my pocket. I surreptitiously slip my hand into my pocket and pat the clue to reassure myself that it's still there. What possessed me to tell Nick I'd wait for him to open it? I don't mind waiting to search for the next clue together, but I am itching to know what the clue *is*. Having this tiny temptation tucked into my pocket is torture.

I take the envelope from my pocket, place it on the desk, and return to the grant documents. But this is no better. If anything, it's worse. Clue No. 4 stares up at me, silently screaming 'open me!' I flip it over. Nope, it's still distracting. Finally, I slide it under my coffee mug and will myself not to look at it.

The afternoon drags on. After three-quarters of an eternity, I estimate it's got to be four, almost five, o'clock. When I look at my watch and see that it's ten minutes after one, I groan. Loudly.

Over in the atrium, Brent Stillwater looks up in surprise from the chessboard where he's in the process of mopping the floor with his grandfather.

"Miss Winters, are you okay?" he squeaks.

Embarrassed by my outburst, I reassure the town's five-year-old chess prodigy that I'm just fine. I check my phone and see a text from Nick:

> Suit needs work. Headed to Ariana's for alterations now. Shouldn't be long.

I text him back 'np,' even thought it's not no problem. It's a big problem called impatience. Then I firmly remind myself that I'm happy that Nick is going to play Santa, he needs his costume to fit in order to do so, and the clue isn't going anywhere. This works. For approximately forty-five seconds.

Before I can second guess myself I snatch the envelope up from under the mug. If I slice open the envelope seal *very* carefully, I could read the clue and reseal the envelope. Nick would never have to know. Besides, this is *my* scavenger hunt. Nick's only tagging along to keep me company—or out of some misguided protective instinct. And, anyway, I'm not going to hunt for the clue without him. What's the harm in a sneaking a peek? It's no different from reading an excerpt of a novel before buying it or watching a movie trailer.

My mental gymnastics have just about convinced me to open the envelope when I hear my name being called from across the library. I drop it like it's radioactive and jerk my head up in time to see two of the three Field sisters heading toward me.

"Hi, Sage. Hi, Thyme." I greet them with a wide smile that I hope looks innocent, or at least not guilty, and maintain steady eye contact with them while I shove the clue back under my coffee mug.

"Hey, Noelle. Isn't it great that Uncle Nick's gonna play Santa for the festival after all?" Sage asks.

"Absolutely!" I chirp.

Thyme cocks her head to study me. "Are you wearing Merry's hoodie?"

"What?" I'm suddenly hyperaware of my borrowed clothes.

"Yeah, that's definitely Merry's. My mom gave it to her for her birthday last year."

Of course. Just my luck. My mind races. How do I explain that I spent the night at the cabin with their uncle without making it sound like I spent the night at the cabin *with* their uncle?

Flustered, I blurt, "Your uncle Nick's helping me with the scavenger hunt. We went looking for a clue this morning. A hike was involved, so I needed to borrow appropriate clothes."

In a serious stroke of luck, the mention of the scavenger hunt distracts them from my attire. They both lean over the desk.

"Another clue? Catch us up."

Happy to oblige, I walk them through finding the clue in the coffee shop, which led me to the lake and Nick. Then I explain how we found the clue in the letterbox up by the waterfall (with a small conversational detour to give them a broad-strokes description of letterboxing). Along the way, they pepper me with questions, talking over each other with rapid-fire speech.

I'm halfway through telling them about the O. Henry clue at Alpine Jewelers, when a gigantic clattering noise fills the first floor. The crashing continues, seemingly endless, until, finally, there's an ear-splitting crescendo.

"Is someone playing cymbals?" Sage asks.

My blood chills as I realize what happened. I hold up one finger. "Wait for it."

Aaaand, there it is. An ear-piercing scream. The sisters instinctively drop into twin fighting stances.

"Will you excuse me? I have to take care of this."

Thyme puts a hand on my arm to stop me before I can dash. "Wait, real quick—Holly said there's a 3D printer here. Sage has this great idea for a party favor."

"Clem!" I point toward the chessboard, and Clemens Still-water looks up. "Can you help Nick Jolly's nieces with the 3D printer?"

He gives me a thumbs up. "Gladly. The kid's trouncing me again, anyway."

I turn back to the sisters. "Clem is our makerspace expert. He'll show you how to use the printer."

Brent giggles and runs over while his grandfather gathers his things. "Come on, I'll take you to the Wonder Workshop. It's upstairs."

As Brent leads them toward the stairs, I race across the lobby and into the children's' wing. I screech to a halt in the middle of the hallway, where Sunny Min sits sobbing in a pile of hundreds of magnetic tiles.

I crouch beside her. "What happened?"

She takes a hiccuping breath, then wails, "Some man knocked over the ball run. And he pushed me down."

I wipe a tear from her cheek. "A man? You're sure he was a grown-up?" Sunny's only six, and she's petite. I'm guessing she means a bigger kid, possibly a preteen.

"A man," she confirms. "He had on a hat and sunglasses. I didn't see his face, but I bet it was a nasty, ugly one."

"He certainly has nasty, ugly behavior," I agree.

She surveys the wreckage. "Why did he do that? We worked so hard."

They did. Sunny and a few of her classmates have been adding to the run every time they visit the library for weeks. The contraption took up half the hallway and was a marvel of elementary school engineering that delighted everyone who sent a ball coursing through it. My heart aches for her and her friends.

"I'm sorry, Sunny. That's very unfair, and if he did it on purpose—"

"He did!" She clenches her tiny fists.

"Okay. Let's get this cleaned up, and then I'll find him and invite him to leave."

She nods. We stack the tiles in the bins that line the wall, then head to the snack room, where a cherry popsicle takes the sting out of the destruction.

After a few licks, her trademark sunshiny grin returns and she sets her jaw in a firm, determined line. "I'm gonna start fixing the ball run, Ms. Winters."

"Yeah?"

"Yep." She gives me a nod. "Sensei Adam says an indomitable spirit is the warrior's greatest weapon."

I make a mental note to let the martial arts teacher know his lessons are sticking, then hold up my palm for a high five. "Go get it, girl."

She slaps my palm, then skips off.

CHAPTER 16

Nick

Ariana's so delighted at the prospect of getting me into my Santa suit that she shoves a beautiful bride and her mother out of the shop, promising to do her dress fitting later.

"Sorry," I mouth as the women gather up their purses to leave.

To my surprise, the bride beams at me. "No problem, Mr. Jolly! We're just glad you're going to be Santa this weekend, after all. It wouldn't be the same without you. Besides, my wedding's not until September."

As they traipse out, Ari hums a Christmas carol under her breath while she flits and flutters around me with the measuring tape. After she promises to have the suit ready to go within the hour, she shoos me out of the shop so she can concentrate.

I wander around the square aimlessly. The crowd is picking up, buzzing with festive energy despite the heat, and I soak in the good vibes. Across the green, there's a long line of people queued up in front of Merry's dessert truck for frozen hot chocolate and homemade peppermint ice cream. Up on the bandstand, the Mapleville Merrymakers, our very own not-entirely-terrible Jimmy Buffett cover band, is playing "Ho Ho Ho and a Bottle of Rhum." A gaggle of kids streaks past me dragging a red sleigh kite behind them, as they search for a breeze.

I lean against a wall near the bookstore and watch the activity for a while, then check my watch. I've killed a grand total of twelve minutes. Now what? I could go back to the house, but Holly and Rosemary are two of a kind, and they've made it abundantly clear that I'm in the way.

I decide to head down to the library. I tell myself this is in the service of efficiency so Noelle and I can open the clue and figure out our next spot while I'm waiting to pick up the suit and not because I want to see her. Then I tell myself that I'm a dirty liar. With a destination in mind, I circle back, hurrying past Ari's Alterations, and head down High Street toward the library.

As I pass in front of Alpine Jewelers, Xander, moving with uncharacteristic alacrity, zips through the front door and grabs me by my collar.

"Nick! I have to show you something." He yanks me into the shop.

I give him a careful look. His eyes are wild, and he's more amped up than I've ever seen him.

"Everything okay, Xander?"

"Come with me."

He tuts at the woman behind the counter, leaving her in charge of the handful of people in the shop, then he leads me to his office in the back. As soon as I walk through the door, he swivels his computer desktop monitor around to face me and stands beside me, jabbing at it.

"Do you see?"

"What are we looking at, Xander?"

"It's the security footage from inside the shop. After you and Noelle left, I couldn't stop thinking about that handprint. It was bothering me."

"I could tell."

"Well, look at this. Just before you two came in, I was helping a family pick out matching charms for their bracelets. It's a tradition." He points to the footage of several women gathered around a display case. He stands behind it, holding a tray of charms in his outstretched hands.

"I see. That's a nice tradition." Where is he going with this?

"The husbands and boyfriends were milling around like bulls waiting to stampede. They were getting antsy, and the shop was getting crowded, so I suggested they visit Merry's truck or the coffee shop. And watch what happens while they're leaving." He points at the monitor at a man who slips through the group. The man tries to and fails to open the locked display window that faces the street.

"Pause it."

He freezes the image. The angle's not great, and the resolution is grainy. In addition, the man is wearing big oversized sunglasses and a baseball cap pulled down low.

"But he wasn't part of that group," Xander continues.

He restarts the recording. The cluster of men streams through the door with the guy in the hat and glasses at the back of the pack. When they reach the sidewalk, the rest of the men turn left, and this man peels off to the right.

"Huh. Can you print a screen capture of him?"

"Sure."

As he hits the button to print the photo, I say, "Do you have security cameras on the back of the building?"

"Of course."

"Have you looked at the footage from behind the shop?"

He shakes his head. "No."

"Can you switch to that camera?"

He clicks some buttons and pulls up the camera feed. It has a view of the bench where Noelle and I sat and a partial view of the alleyway between his building and the next one.

"All right, cue it up to the time when that man left."

He fusses with the keys, and I lean in. We see nothing but an empty courtyard for a while. The guy in the hat and sunglasses appears at the edge of the alleyway. As we watch, he crosses the yard on a diagonal, heading toward the library.

"Can you—?"

"Should I call the county police?" Xander cuts me off, interrupting someone for what may well be the first time in his life.

I consider my answer. "Nothing's missing, right?"

"No. But he's up to something."

"Oh, no doubt." I agree. "But if you can hold off for a

couple hours, I'll circle back with Noelle and see if we can figure out what's going on. We haven't opened the clue yet. It might give us some ideas."

He mulls it over for several seconds, then nods, and hands me the printout. "I can do that."

"Thanks."

I've got my hand on the doorknob to leave when he says, "By the way, I heard Josh had to leave town. I'm glad you're getting back in the Santa saddle."

Me, too. But before I can engage Santa mode in earnest, I need to figure out what the man in the video is up to.

CHAPTER 17

Noelle

After a thorough search of all three floors, I haven't come across a man wearing a hat and sunglasses, and none of the patrons remembers seeing anyone who matches the description. I lean against the railing at the top of the stairs to thumb out a quick email to Sunny's parents to let them know what happened. Then I forward a copy to the entire library staff, asking everyone to keep an eye out for the misanthropic menace.

Stymied for now and unsettled by the rotten behavior, I head back to the desk and I pick up my mug for a much-needed swig of what's probably lukewarm coffee. It's halfway to my lips when I realize the envelope it was holding down is gone.

"No, no, no, no, no."

Maybe I unthinkingly put it back in my pocket? I shove my hand in to check, but it's empty. As a rule, I pride myself on not cursing in the library, but I am very, very close to letting loose a stream of profanity that would make even Griselda blush. I drop to my knees and search under my desk.

When I hear my name being called, I pop up and promptly bang my head on the underside of the desk. I yelp, then back out, rubbing my head, and turn around to see Sage and Thyme.

"Check out the prototype!" Sage triumphantly holds up a small plastic mistletoe sprig with two berries on top. The ornament dangles from a red- and white-striped length of fabric ribbon.

"Cute." I manage a vague smile, my mind still on the missing envelope.

"Right? We're going to use them as personalized wine tags at the happy hour tomorrow, and then the guests can take them home and hang them up!" Thyme beams.

Sage narrows her eyes. "What's wrong?"

"What?"

"Your face is so white it's almost see-through. And you're sweating," she informs me.

I swipe my hand across my forehead and my palm comes away wet. Eww.

I groan, " I lost the new clue."

They both gasp.

"But you've already read it. Right?" Thyme asks in a hopeful voice.

I stick out my lip and shake my head. "I told Nick we'd open it together after he gets his suit sorted out. So I put it right here under my coffee mug for safekeeping."

"And it's not there now?"

"Right. I left it there when I went to deal with that ear-splitting noise earlier."

"What *was* that, anyway?" Sage wants to know.

"Several hundred magnetic tiles crashing to the ground. Some jerk knocked it down deliberately and then *pushed* a little girl. After I got poor Sunny settled down and we cleaned up the mess, I scoured the entire library looking for the buttwipe who did it. But I couldn't find him."

"May his pillowcase always be warm and his coffee room temperature," Thyme mutters darkly.

I raise a questioning eyebrow.

Sage explains, "It's one of our mom's favorite curses."

"Brutal."

"MJ doesn't play."

Thyme butts in. "How long were you away from the desk?"

"As long as you were, I guess." I check my watch. "Almost half an hour. I just got back here. When I picked up my coffee mug, the envelope was gone."

"And you're sure you didn't move it?" Sage asks.

"I did *not* move it," I say firmly.

"Huh. Well, it must be here somewhere. We'll help you look for it."

They join me behind the circulation desk. We methodi-cally search every inch of the space, each nook and individual cranny. In the end, Thyme finds it tucked into the tray of monthly calendars on display for visitors to grab after checking out their books. My relief is dampened by my conviction that I did not put it there. I. Did. Not. Put. It. There.

Judging by the looks I'm getting from the sisters, I said that part aloud.

"Well, I didn't."

"Maybe it fluttered off your desk, someone picked it up. and stuck it in the tray thinking they were being helpful," Thyme theorizes.

I look around the circulation desk for this mysterious, helpful person, then I shrug.

"Maybe. I guess it doesn't matter because it's here now."

"Right," she agrees.

They're both staring at me expectantly.

"What?"

"Open it," they urge in unison.

"I told you, I promised your uncle we'd open it together."

"Pfft." Sage's dismissal of my commitment is both short and eloquent.

Thyme takes a slightly softer approach. "He'll understand. Besides, you *owe* us. We helped you find it. I mean, technically, *I* found it."

They're giving me an excuse to do what I want to do.

"Oh, what the heck. Let's do it." I grab my letter opener from the pen holder on my desk and slit the envelope open.

They crowd in close and lean over my shoulders to read it along with me: *Go to the place where you'll find ladies dancing and lords a-leaping.* I frown down at the words.

Sage nudges me. "What's wrong? You look irritated."

"It's from 'The Twelve Days of Christmas,'" Thyme says helpfully. "Days Nine and Ten."

"Yeah. I know. It's just not very original. Another clue from the same song? Plus it's very on the nose."

"Who knew you were so fussy and particular about your completely surprise, gifted scavenger hunts?" Thyme snarks.

"Well, when you put it like that, I do sound a smidge ungrateful."

"You said it's on the nose. Does that mean you know where it is?"

"Sure do."

They stare at me with expectant expressions. I draw out the moment until Thyme starts tapping her toe.

"Noelle," she warns.

"It's Dancing Ladies."

"Which is?"

"Which is exactly what it sounds like—an establishment where ladies dance."

"A night club?" Sage asks.

"No. A strip club."

"I believe those are called gentlemen's clubs," she corrects me.

"Well, the guys who frequent this club may be lords, but I have no idea if they're gentlemen."

I'm met by two blank stares.

"The Lords of the Mountain is a motorcycle club. My understanding is Dancing Ladies is their hangout or head-quarters or what have you."

"Mistletoe Mountain has its own biker gang?"

I flash to the Christmas in July parade, led each year by the

Lords, one of whom pulls a sidecar filled with toys they collect for the charity. "I don't know that they're a *gang*, exactly."

It must be my imagination, but I could swear they look disappointed.

"Still, I wish we could come with you. But we have a lot of mistletoe favors to make, and Clem says they're going to take at least fifteen minutes each to print." Sage frowns. "Are you going to wait for Uncle Nick to go to this club?"

"Of course. I told him I would."

They exchange a look. "What?"

"Merry told us you two used to date."

Heat creeps up my neck to my cheeks. "I didn't realize Nick told his daughters."

"He didn't," she informs me. "Aunt Carol did."

"Oh. Well, yes, I guess you could say we dated. Briefly. A very long time ago. In college. We met when we were both doing internships in London." Am I overexplaining? I feel as if I might be overexplaining, so I clamp my mouth shut.

"Right. Mom and Dad wanted him to get some real-world experience because he was supposed to come help them run the resort."

Sage says, "I wish he had gone to work for them at Tranquility by the Sea. Then maybe it wouldn't have ended up the way it did."

I don't know the details, but over the years, I've heard the broad strokes. Nick's sister and her husband ended up in some financial trouble with both the IRS and a loan shark, and the three sisters have been digging out from under it.

I nod sympathetically. Then I point out, "Of course, if he'd have done that, he never would have met your Aunt Carol. And you wouldn't have your cousins." *And he wouldn't be back in my life.*

Thyme agrees, "True. And if our parents hadn't mishandled the resort, I wouldn't have met Victor, Sage wouldn't have met Roman, and Rosemary wouldn't be Mrs. Detective Dave. I can't even imagine that alternate reality."

"So you guys *were* a couple," Sage says, bringing us back to the topic at hand—a topic I have exactly zero desire to explore with Nick's nieces.

"We had a summer romance, and then it was over. It was time- and location-limited."

They both cock their heads, confused.

I try again. "Imagine a world without email, video chat, social media, and texting. No cell phones." As they continue to look at me blankly, I explain, "I know it probably defies understanding, but in the last millennium things were different. When the summer ended, we were an ocean apart. And airmail isn't the straightest path to a sustainable relationship."

"So it … fizzled out?" Sage asks.

"Exactly. And, after it fizzled out, your uncle came back to the States for his senior year, but I stayed. I transferred to Oxford to finish up. Then, after I graduated I did a year-long traineeship. Then I moved to Italy to do a master's program. Meanwhile, your Uncle Nick graduated and got a job at the inn in my old hometown, which he'd heard me talk about so fondly. And that's how he met Carol."

They digest this.

Then Thyme draws her eyebrows together. "So you didn't know they were together, Aunt Carol didn't know you and

Uncle Nick had been together, and he didn't know you and Aunt Carol had been childhood besties? That's wild."

"Remember, it's not as if we were all posting selfies and updates on Picagram and FacePlace back then. The most surprising thing, really, is that Carol tracked me down and asked me to be her maid of honor. My parents had retired to Arizona by then, so she had to do some digging to get an address for me in Ravenna."

"She wrote you *a letter* to tell you she was getting married?"

"Yep. I still have it somewhere. She went on and on about this amazing guy but never said his name." A slow smile spreads across my face at the memory. "So I didn't know *who* she was marrying until I walked into their engagement party and saw your uncle."

Thyme shakes her head in disbelief.

Sage asks, "Was it *so* awkward?"

I answer honestly. "It was a surprise. But, it had been two, almost three, years since I'd seen Nick. And your aunt was my best friend on the planet. I was happy for her. I was happy for him, too."

"And you were living the life in Italy."

"Right." I hope my tone doesn't convey the utter lie of this statement.

"Still, it's such a great story. Why did the three of you keep it a secret from Holly, Ivy, and Merry for so long?"

"I don't think anyone meant to keep it a secret. Honestly, your aunt and uncle probably both thought it wasn't worth mentioning to your cousins because, it was just a summer fling."

They exchange a look.

"What?"

"Toward the end, I guess Aunt Carol had a different perspective," Thyme answers slowly and then falls silent.

I turn to Sage, who says, "She told the cousins about you and Uncle Nick because she thought you might end up together after she was gone. She wanted them to understand your history."

My stomach drops and I open my mouth, but no words come out.

Sage babbles, "We shouldn't have said anything. I'm sorry. You know, she was on a lot of pain medication. She was probably just, confused, or maybe they misunderstood."

"No, it's fine. It's really nothing," I lie lamely.

"Right." They give each other another worried look.

"Really," I insist.

After an awkward moment, Sage says, "Well, I guess we should get back to the workshop and help the Stillwaters print the rest of these ornaments."

"Is it okay if we monopolize your printer for the next few hours?" Thyme asks.

I drop into my chair, give a vague wave toward the stairs, and mumble, "Yeah, go ahead."

They leave, and I lower my head into my hands, mortified.What was Carol thinking? Did she really believe I've spent the past twenty-five years pining for her husband? Then an even worse, more humiliating thought rises up. What if she said as much to Nick? What if he thinks I showed up at the cabin because I have feelings for him?

I let out a strangled groan and lift my head. My gaze falls

on the clue. Finding the next clue will take my mind off this embarrassing mess, and there's no way I'm sticking around to face Nick now. I grab the note card from the desk and call over to Farah, who's helping a patron check out a wood chisel from the tool library, that I have to run an errand. Then I race out the back door to the parking lot.

CHAPTER 18

Nick

I scour the library for Noelle. She's not behind the circulation desk. I check her office, the kitchen, and the children's wing, pausing for a moment to watch little Sunny Min carefully constructing some sort of towering tile structure. No Noelle.

I retrace my steps to the lobby and stop in front of the bulletin board to pull out my phone and text her. A magazine article hanging on the board catches my eye. There's a picture of Noelle, beaming, as she cuts a red ribbon with a pair of ridiculously oversized scissors at the grand opening of the new children's wing. I scan the text. Apparently, she put Griselda's donation to good use. According to the article, the design and philosophy behind her revamped program garnered international recognition in the library world for its 'holistic, integrated approach to child and adolescent development through community spaces.'

My chest fills with an irrational swell of pride for her. Looks like she was right—our little town is big enough to hold her big dreams, after all.

"Uncle Nick! Yoo-hoo!"

I look up to see Sage hanging over the railing outside the Wonder Workshop on the second floor. I wave back and mount the stairs to join her.

"What are you doing here?"

She displays a mistletoe dangling from a ribbon, then jerks a thumb toward the glass wall behind her. "Clem Stillwater and his grandson are helping me and Thyme 3D-print favors for the open house. See?"

I wave to Thyme and the Stillwaters inside the workshop, then lean forward to examine the ornament. "Very nice. Have you seen Noelle?"

Her eyes light up. "Oh, are you ready to go to the strip club?"

I mean, that's what it *sounds* like she says. I'm obviously mishearing her. I shake my head like a wet dog. "Come again?"

"Crud." She clamps a hand over her mouth.

Watching us through the glass, Thyme seems to sense trouble. She slips out the door to join us.

"Did you tell him she opened the clue without him?" she hisses at her sister through clenched teeth.

Sage screws up her face in an apologetic expression.

"Never mind that. What's this about a strip club?"

Thyme sighs heavily. "Noelle said the clue directed her to a place called Dancing Ladies."

"Really?"

"Yeah, it said something like 'go to the place where there are lords a-leaping and ladies dancing.'"

I frown. "That does definitely point to Dancing Ladies." But it feels wrong. "I'm surprised whoever set up the hunt used the same song twice. There must be a thousand Christmas carols to choose from."

Sage nods in agreement. "That's what Noelle said, too. She called it unoriginal and on the nose."

"Hmm. Do you know where she is? She's not at the desk."

They exchange a look.

"That's where she was the last time we saw her," Thyme says.

"Maybe she went to look for the guy in the hat and sunglasses again?" Sage suggests.

Until this moment, I thought 'my blood runs cold' was just a saying. But, turns out, it's not. My blood runs cold.

"Who?" My voice is hard.

They both rear their heads back and give me wide-eyed looks.

"Um, some guy knocked down this tile thing a little girl was building. Then he pushed her. She told Noelle he was wearing a baseball hat and pair of sunglasses. She's been on a mission to find him," Sage explains tentatively.

Thyme jumps in. "That's why she opened the clue, Uncle Nick. While she was looking for the jerk, the envelope with the clue went missing. We helped her find it and begged her to open it. She wanted to wait for you, but we were pretty relentless. Sorry."

I wave off the apology. "It's fine. Don't worry about that. I need to find her right away."

Adrenaline pounds through my veins. It can't be a coincidence that the man from the jewelry store turned up here. Or that the clue, at least temporarily, disappeared. Or that someone was in the woods. Or. Or. Or. My mind races.

I turn and look down over the railing to the first floor, swiveling my head until I spot Farah. I whip back around to my nieces. "I'll see you back at the inn later." I leave them standing there and take the stairs two at a time to the ground floor.

"Farah!" I shout as I run over to her.

Startled, she jumps. "Mr. Jolly? Is everything okay?"

I ignore the question. "Where's Noelle?"

She smooths her headscarf with one hand and gives me a worried look. "She had to run an errand."

"Did she say where she was going?"

"No."

She wouldn't have gone to Dancing Ladies alone. Would she? Even as I have the thought, I know she would, and did. I have to go there. Now. My racing mind screeches to a halt as I remember that Noelle drove us into town. My truck is miles away at the fishing cabin.

I eye Farah for a moment. Then I say, "Can I borrow your car?"

It's a big ask, but the teenager doesn't hesitate. She reaches into her pocket for her keys.

"Sure. But, just so you know, it's running on fumes. I was supposed to get gas on my way to work but there was a line, and I didn't want to be late."

"I'll fill it up," I tell her. "As a thank you."

She grins and drops the keys into my palm. "Awesome." Her eyes spark and her hand returns to her pocket. "Wait. Take this, too." She pulls out a sealed envelope labeled *Clue No. 4* and holds it out to me.

I take it and study it for a moment. Turning it over, I confirm that it's unopened. "Where did you get this?"

"Noelle must have dropped it. I guess someone picked it up and threw it away. Brent Stillwater found it in the wastepaper basket in the restroom and brought it to me."

"Thanks." Then I frown. "What was he doing going through the bathroom trash?"

She drops her voice to a whisper. "I don't mean to be unkind, Mr. Jolly. I understand he's a genius or whatever, but he's an unusual little kid. Who knows why he does *anything*?"

"Fair enough." I pocket the clue and head toward the back of the building. Then I remember I don't know what she drives and turn on my heel. "What's your ride?"

"It's the white Nissan Altima parked at the end of the lot. Look for the pink cheetah print steering wheel cover." She shares this information with a proud smile.

"Okay … thanks. I guess."

As I run out the door, I remind myself beggars can't be choosers and that, as a girl dad, I've driven worse. The Tuscadaro pink Jeep Wrangler Merry had in high school, for instance.

I repeat this reminder when I cram myself behind the wheel of Farah's car, turn the key in the ignition, and have my eardrums nearly blown out by blaring K-pop music. And, again when the fuel indicator warning light confirms that I'll be lucky to make it to the gas station before the little sedan runs out of gas.

By some miracle, I coast down Silver Bell Lane to the nearest filling station and putter to an open fuel pump. As I fill the tank, I tap my foot and will the gas to flow faster. I don't know exactly what's going on, but this much, I do know: Noelle shouldn't be out roaming alone while a strange guy's lurking around town. The pump clicks off, and I jump back in the car and pull out like I'm being chased.

I'm coming, Noe. Don't do anything stupid.

CHAPTER 19

Noelle

I sit in my car, my attention shifting from the map unfolded on my lap to the ramshackle shack with the drooping fairy lights strung along the roof. Dancing Ladies isn't much to look at from the outside. I have a suspicion it's not much to look at from the inside either, but I don't have any firsthand knowledge to support this guess.

I'm stalling. I've been sitting here for twenty minutes even though the clue is glaringly obvious. This has to be the spot. It's right there in the name. And the row of motorcycles parked to the right of the metal doors at the entrance might as well be a big, blinking arrow. The Lords of the Mountain are here. I don't know if they're leaping, exactly, but this is the right place. It has to be.

Still, I hesitate. Aside from being a skosh nervous about

strolling into a nudie bar frequented by a gang of bikers, I'm hung up on one detail. Dancing Ladies isn't technically on the map. The spot where I sit *is* on the map, but there's no structure marked. So far, all the clues have been in places that are represented on the map. Even the waterfall and the big rock outcropping are drawn in. But not this strip club. And, technically, according to the signage on Hemlock Road, it's just over the county line. I'm not in Mistletoe Mountain anymore, Toto.

"Stop being a chicken." I say it aloud in an effort to convince myself to get moving.

I must be persuasive, because I fold up the map and return it to my glove box. Then I exit the car, tugging my hoodie down over the form-fitting yoga pants to cover my bum as I march toward the front door of the club. I reassure myself that no one's going to be checking out my butt or any other part of my anatomy when the competition is flexible women who dance for a living. I take a deep breath, wrap my fingers around the sticky handle of the front door, and try not to imagine what substance might account for the stickiness as I give the door a push. I consider wiping my hand on my jacket and think better of it. Then I plunge into what I'm sure will be the dank, dark, dirty, and depressing interior of Dancing Ladies.

I stop just inside the door and blink. It's none of these things. The decrepit exterior hides an open, airy room. Velvet settees and overstuffed chairs are scattered throughout the space in cozy groupings. A long, gleaming bar runs the length of one wall. Strings of tiny lights twinkle along the ceiling. It's prettier than I'd expected.

There are, however, bikers everywhere. At first glance, they're intimidating. Leather vests with no shirts underneath, tattoos, and heavy boots. Loud, raucous laughter and shouted conversations. But on closer inspection, I recognize several of the Lords. I spot the town orthodontist, the swim instructor from the pool, my insurance agent, and Brent Stillwater's dad, who runs an animal rescue center.

Shifting my focus from the patrons to the performers, I see several women I recognize from Griselda's studio. There are two satellite stages and a larger main stage. The dancers are not naked—they're what I would call *lightly* clothed. And judging by their hip gyrations, none of them get called out during Hoop It Up class.

I sidle up to the bar. After a moment, I catch the bartender's eye. He's a young guy, built like a linebacker, with close-cropped hair and an earring sparkling in one ear.

"What's your poison?"

Just then, the music pulsing from the speakers hits a bridge and I have to shout, "Soda water with a twist of lime."

He throws me a wink and mouths, "You got it."

I'm trying to figure out the best way to ask this man if he has a clue for me when someone taps my shoulder.

"Ms. Winters?"

I turn around to see Delphina Gupta gawking at me. I gape back at her, as surprised as she is. "Noelle. If there's ever a place that you should call me by my first name, it's here."

She tips back her head and laughs. "What are *you* doing here?"

I wonder the same about her. But it's not my business, so I say, "Looking for a clue."

"Here?" She instantly hones in on the issue. "I don't remember this place being on your map."

"It's not. But this has to be the right spot." I pull out the clue and hand it to her.

She studies it with a small frown before passing it back to me. "You're right. But why isn't it on the map?"

I tuck the clue away and then throw my hands wide, palms up. "Beats me."

The bartender returns with my drink and raises an eyebrow at Delphina. "Another round of tequila for your table?"

"Please."

"Ah, youth," I snort.

She shrugs. "Sometimes a girl needs to break free of the Christmas-all-the-time vibe in town. Don't get me wrong, I love Mistletoe Mountain, but it's … a lot."

I can only imagine. Sometimes it's a lot for me, and I grew up here. Delphina's parents moved to Vermont from Bangalore when she was two years old. And while Mistletoe Mountain celebrates every holiday under the sun, from Diwali to Holi, Hanukkah to Eid-al-Fitr, and throws a lunar new year festival and a Pride Parade that must be seen to be believed, it remains a relentlessly, unapologetically Christmassy town. Who am I to judge if she wants to take off her elf hat for a night and cut loose?

"I get it," I assure her.

The bartender returns with four shots. After Delphina settles up, I help her carry the drinks over to her table. She introduces me to her friends, who urge me to join them, but she waves them off.

"I'll be right back," she tells them. She motions for me to follow her. "Come on."

We head back to the bar, and she leans across the surface to shout, "Titus, did anybody leave a message for my friend? Her name is Noelle."

His eyes slide over my face as he answers her. "I don't think anyone expected your friend to be here."

"That's fair. How about any messages for anybody?"

Titus' expression tightens. "It's not that kind of place, Delphina. The Lords are super clear about that—no dealing, no arranging deals. That's not what we're doing here."

"No, it's nothing like that," I reassure him. "I'm doing a scavenger hunt, and my last clue brought me here."

"Sorry, ma'am. I don't know what kind of scavenger hunt you're doing, but whatever you're looking for, it's not here. Unless it's in the bottom of a glass or up on the stage."

I'm offended that he called me *ma'am* and disappointed that he doesn't have an envelope tucked behind the bar for me.

Deflated, I drop my shoulders. "Okay, thanks."

He walks to the other end of the bar to wait on a cluster of patrons.

Delphina shakes her head. "This *has* to be the clue."

I scan the room. I can't quite see myself crawling under all these tables and searching for an envelope. "I don't know …"

She snaps her fingers. "There's a seating area out back—some picnic tables, and a porta-john. They have live music on the weekends. Maybe it's out on the patio."

"Maybe," I say, not very hopefully. "I'll check it out on my way out. Enjoy your evening."

She reaches for my arm. "Wait. Please don't say anything to Holly or her family about, you know, what I said about Christmas."

I glance over her head and nod toward a group of Lords who also belong to the Chamber of Commerce. "Your secret's safe with me, but I'm pretty sure everyone in town has thought at least once of trading Christmas all year for something slightly edgier."

She laughs. "Thanks for understanding."

She makes her way back to her friends and tosses back her shot. I dig into the zippered pocket of the yoga pants and smooth out the emergency ten dollar bill I tucked in there earlier. I slip it under my glass.

"Thanks," the bartender calls, jerking his chin at me while he pulls two pints from the beer taps. "Good luck with your search. I hope you find what you're looking for."

As I cross the floor to the door, the song ends. In the sudden silence, I can feel eyes boring into my back. I pick up my pace. The music resumes as I nudge the door open.

I step out into the parking lot and pause to look for a path to the back patio. I spot it on the other side of the building. As I pass by the line of motorcycles, the door opens and someone else leaves the club with a burst of music. I round the corner of the building and head for the patio.

Judging by the crunch of the gravel behind me, instead of continuing on to their bike or car, the person who followed me out the door is trailing me to the back of the building. Even though it's still daylight, my heart rate ticks up and the skin on the back of my neck prickles just like it did in the woods yesterday. I dig my car keys out of my pocket, fist them between my fingers, teeth out, and quicken my pace.

Just a quick search of the picnic tables, I promise myself.

Even as I try to pretend that I'm not in danger, part of my brain is screaming at me. If I were reading this in one of my mystery books, I would be disgusted and frustrated by the main character's questionable decision-making. There's a decent chance I'd slam my book shut in frustration, declaring the sleuth in question TSTL—too stupid to live.

I walk even faster, almost jogging now. The footsteps behind me speed up, too. Should I turn around and make eye contact, let my pursuer know I know they're there? Or should I just keep going, not engage? Before I have a chance to decide, a hand wraps around my upper arm, yanks me off the path, and pulls me behind the porta-potty.

There are two of them.

The realization hits me like a flash—along with the terrifying thought that I really might be too stupid to live.

I fill my lungs, then pierce the air with a scream that gets cut off as a heavy hand clamps over my mouth.

CHAPTER 20

Nick

Noelle thrashes and writhes wildly in my arms, struggling to break free. As I lean forward to tell her she's safe, she suddenly jerks her head up and wedges her upper lip above the top of my palm. She bites down hard on the fleshy, sensitive webbing between my thumb and forefinger. Really hard.

Son of a Blitzen.

I grit my teeth to keep from yelling. Then I press my mouth against her ear and whisper, "It's me—Nick."

She relaxes instantly, going limp in my arms. I pull her further up the hillside where we'll be concealed from view by the scrubby brushes at the edge of the property. Once I'm sure we're out of sight, I ease us both down to the ground. She sags back against my chest. I feel her shoulders shaking and wrap my arms around her in a tight embrace.

"Shh, shh." I press my lips to the crown of her head and soothe her until her quivering stops.

She takes a shuddering breath then wraps her fingers lightly my hand and holds it up to her face to inspect my bite wound. Her touch is warm and gentle.

"I broke the skin. I'm sorry."

"You were scared, and you didn't know it was me. It was a good reaction," I tell her, and I mean it. She started fighting right away, like it was muscle memory. "Where'd you learn that move?"

She twists around to look at me. "Sensei Adam's Sunday morning adult self-defense class. I go with some of the book club crew and then we have a boozy brunch at the Tipsy Turnip."

"Good. Keep going to that self-defense class." I make a note to tell my daughters I'll pay for the three of them to take the class, too.

Her bright green eyes fill with remorse. "But I hurt you."

"Eh." I wave it off. "Not unless you have rabies. You don't have rabies, do you?"

"Not to my knowledge." She giggles.

"Then, it's all good."

Her smile fades and her expression grows serious again. "I think someone was following me."

"Someone was. I watched a man come out of the club a few seconds behind you and trail you back here. So I got out of the car and ran around the other side of the building to intercept you."

"Did you get a look at him?"

I lower my chin and give her a long, serious look. "He was wearing a baseball hat and big sunglasses."

She blanches. "Where did he go?"

"When I pulled you off the trail, he'd nearly caught up to you. He saw me and took off toward the parking lot. I'm sure he's long gone by now."

Maybe I should have chased him instead of grabbing her. But my priority isn't catching this dickhead, it's keeping her safe. When I saw him skulking behind her, I wasn't filled with a white-hot alpha male urge to bash his face in. No, every cell of my body screamed for me to scoop her up and take her to safety. It was a clarion call to protect her. So I did.

"Thank goodness you were here." She rests her cheek on my chest and takes a deep breath. "Why *are* you here though?"

"Let me see the clue."

She frowns at the nonanswer but digs into the pocket on the side of her yoga pants and pulls it out. I take the clue Farah gave me and hold them side by side. They're similar, but they aren't the same. Noelle's envelope is slightly wider and the ivory color is off by a shade.

"Thanks. Do you have one of the other clues?"

She reaches into her pocket again and takes out Clue No. 3 —the one that led us to Xander's jewelry store.

I pluck it from between her fingers and hold it beside the others. "Look. The envelope and paper from Clue No. 3 don't match your Clue No. 4. They match mine."

"Where did you get that?"

"Farah gave it to me when I came to the library looking for you. She said the Stillwater boy found it in one of the bathrooms."

She shakes her head. "I don't understand."

"He switched the clues, Noelle. The guy in the hat and sunglasses. The one you looked all over the library for."

Her eyes widen with sudden understanding. "That whole scene—knocking over the ball run, pushing Sunny down—that was a distraction to get me away from the desk so he could take the real clue and replace it with this fake one."

"And lure you up here." I say it gently, but she has to hear it. She needs to connect the dots.

She buries her face in my shirt collar. "Why would someone want to lure me anywhere? Does he want to hurt me?"

My pulse thuds, and I suppress the urge to growl at the pain and fear in her voice. I force myself to speak in a measured tone. "I don't know if he wants to hurt you, but he's definitely been following you throughout the scavenger hunt."

She pushes her hands against my chest, leans back, and meets my eyes. "How can you know that?"

I take out the grainy image Xander printed, unfold and smooth it out, then hand it to her. The paper shakes in her hands as she stares down at it.

"Where did you get this?"

"Xander."

She lifts her head and arches an eyebrow. "Xander?"

"He grabbed me when I was on my way to the library. He wanted to show me his security camera footage."

"Why?"

"He was worried about that handprint on his display case. And he was right to worry." I jab the page with my finger.

"This guy was messing around with the display case that holds the pocket watch chain and the hair combs."

"He wanted to switch the clues before we got there, but the case was locked," she says, working through the scenario aloud.

"Right. So he moved on to Plan B. He caused an uproar at the library and then switched them while you were helping Sunny."

"We need to go inside," she says forcefully.

I eye the strip club skeptically. "I don't know, Noelle. I doubt anyone in there knows this dude and—"

"No, Delphina's in there."

"Really?"

She ignores my surprise. "When I went to the coffee shop to get the first clue, I thought it was empty. I was there during the afternoon lull and I didn't see anyone. But somebody was there. I heard the bell when they left. Delphina said it was a guy wearing a pair of oversized sunglasses and a baseball hat pulled down low over his forehead, covering his face. She joked about him being a movie star hiding from the paparazzi."

My skin heats. This guy's been following her from the beginning. My expression must speak volumes because she swallows hard and stares at me.

"You think it's the same guy, don't you? He was probably the person who we heard in the woods."

"Do you have Delphina's phone number?" I say. "It's better if she comes out here. If we go in there, the Lords are going to want to get involved."

Our local motorcycle club, made up of accountants, family

men, and grocery story clerks cosplaying as Sons of Anarchy, likes to step in and fill the role that a police department fills in other towns.

She nods and pulls out her phone. Her thumbs fly over the keyboard as she types out a quick message. After she stows the phone back in her pocket, I take her hand and lead her down to the parking lot. When we reach the gravel parking pad, I loosen my grasp to release her hand, but she laces her fingers tightly between mine instead.

She cocks her head when she sees Farah's little white sedan parked next to her car. "You borrowed Farah's car?"

"My truck's up at the cabin, remember?"

"Right." She shakes her head like she's disappointed in herself for forgetting a minor detail in the middle of this scat storm. "How'd you find me, though?"

I'm explaining that I ran into Sage and Thyme when the club's metal door opens, and Delphina marches out. She swivels her head toward us, and Noelle lifts her hand in a small wave.

Delphina jogs over. "Hey, Mr. Jolly!"

I give my oldest daughter's lifelong best friend a probing look. "Holly doesn't come out here, does she?"

She snorts. "Could you imagine Holly here? Especially with *Anderson*?"

She laces the name with disdain. Noelle wrinkles her nose at the mention of Holly's fiancé.

They aren't wrong. Anderson Wilson Carson, Esquire, is a gigantic pain in the tinsel, and, while he might be the right match for some poor soul, he and Holly go together like eggnog and ketchup. But we all know one immutable fact about Holly—the more you push, the more she pulls. So we're following the game plan Carol devised when young Anderson slipped that oversized rock on our daughter's finger: be entirely, infuriatingly neutral about him and wait for Holly to snap to her senses. Then pick up the pieces.

This war of attrition doesn't prohibit us from indulging in some light snark about the guy. "Actually, I'd love to see Anderson here. The Lords would have a field day with him."

Delphina chuckles.

Noelle brings us back to the task at hand. "Listen, you two, as much as I'd love to engage in a speed round of 'Anderson Sucks Eggs,' we do have a more pressing issue."

"Right, sorry. What's up?" Delphina snaps to attention.

"Do you remember the man who was in the coffee shop yesterday when I came in looking for the clue?" Noelle asks.

"Oh, sure, Mr. Incognito. For a guy trying to go unnoticed, he sure is memorable."

Noelle hands her the image. "This isn't a great picture, but is this him?"

She squints at it for a long moment. "I *think* so." After a beat, she says, "Yeah, it's him."

"Thanks," I tell her.

She hands the paper back and asks, "Is this part of your scavenger hunt? Did you find the next clue?"

"Maybe," Noelle says weakly.

I chime in, "Thanks for your help, Delphina. We won't keep you from your friends any longer."

She gives Noelle a searching look, then shrugs. "Okay. Have fun with your scavenger hunt."

As Delphina heads back to the strip club, I call after her,

"And if you don't have a designated driver, call the Sober Sleigh for a ride home!"

Without turning around, she waves her hand over her head in acknowledgment.

I shift my attention to Noelle, who's staring down at the real, unopened clue. "This is your party, so you get to pick. We can head out to the sheriff's department and report this guy or we can continue the scavenger hunt with the understanding that you do not take off on your own again. That means if we have to put it aside until I take care of Santa-related business, you wait."

She exhales, long and slow. "This guy, whoever he is, is a creep and a jerk. But as far as I know, it's not against the law to sabotage a scavenger hunt."

"So you're choosing Option B?"

"Option B," she confirms.

"And no freelancing."

"No freelancing," she parrots dutifully.

I give her a grin and gesture toward the envelope. "What are you waiting for, then? Open it."

CHAPTER 21

Noelle

My stomach is jumpy, my pulse is fluttery, and my heart is a drum. I need a mug of chamomile tea and a bubble bath. But what I have is a stalker and a scavenger hunt.

And a protector. I eye Nick. By rights, he should be at the inn getting ready for the weekend. Stocking the bar or practicing "ho, ho, hos" in the mirror. Or something. Instead, he's appointed himself my guardian angel. And judging by his wide-legged defensive stance and fisted hands, not to mention the steel in his hazel eyes, he's taking this job way too seriously.

"Open it," he urges.

Right. The clue. I tear into the envelope making no effort to open it neatly. He leans closer to read the note over my shoulder, and his scent—somehow spicy and pine-fresh at the same time—fills my nose. I take what I hope is a subtle sniff and try to focus on the clue rather than the man brushing against my shoulder. It's basically an impossible task.

You're nearly done. Your final clue signals when an angel gets his wings.

I feel my brow scrunching up as I stare down at the words. Nick's proximity must be scrambling my brain cells, because I've got nothing. I'm clueless, as it were.

I look up at him. "Any ideas?"

He drops his chin and gapes at me. "You're kidding, right?"

I read the clue again. What am I missing? I return my attention to his face.

"No, I'm not kidding. I have no idea what this one means." I try to concentrate. "An angel, apparently a male one. Maybe the topper on the tree in the town square? That's an angel, isn't it?"

He's shaking his head before I even finish the sentence. "No. For one thing, the tree topper in December is an angel; the July tree topper is an *angelfish*."

Right. The summer tree is decorated with, well, summery things.

"Oh, yeah." I twist my mouth to the side and think.

He continues, "Besides, it's obvious what this clue means. It's the easiest one."

I throw my hands wide. "Obviously it's not obvious to me. Care to enlighten me?"

"It's from *It's a Wonderful Life.* You know, the Jimmy Stewart movie."

"Okay, so what's it mean?"

He's side-eyeing me now. "You've seen the movie, right?"

"No. Actually, I haven't."

I wait for the reaction that this admission has garnered more than once over the years. There it is. His jaw hinges open and his eyes bug out.

"You haven't seen *It's a Wonderful Life*?"

"Correct."

"How is that possible? How is it possible in general, but also, how could you have grown up in *this* town and not watched *that* movie at least once? The Mistletoe Movie House runs it every December."

I shrug. "I don't know, Nick. I just haven't. But you clearly have. So, what does the clue mean?"

He shakes his head, marveling at this gap in my Christmas knowledge. "At the end of the movie, Zuzu says—"

"Zuzu?"

"George Bailey's little girl." He raises both eyebrows. "Stewart plays George Bailey."

"Okay, what does Zuzu say?"

"There's a bell ornament hanging on the Christmas tree in the scene, and it starts to ring. Zuzu points to it and says 'every time a bell rings, an angel gets his wings.'"

I consider this. "So we need to find a bell hanging on a tree? Or just any bell?"

There must be dozens of bells in town. Maybe hundreds. A bell dangles over the entrance of every storefront. The preschool has a handbell choir, which is every bit as chaotic as it sounds. There's a bell on the circulation desk at the library —a round brass bell like the ones hotel front desks used to have.

He interrupts my mental inventory of bells. "Did you bring the map?"

"Yep." I unlock my passenger side door and lean in to retrieve it from my glove compartment.

We smooth it out on the hood of my car. He jabs a finger. "There."

He's pointing to the Candlelight Chapel right in the middle of town. It has an open belfry, so I can see the logic, but it's not the no-brainer he's making it out to be.

"Couldn't it just as easily be one of the churches? Or even the courthouse? The chapel isn't the only bell tower in town."

"True, but it's the chapel. I know it is."

He's probably right. In addition to being Mistletoe Mountain's go-to wedding spot, the nondenominational chapel gets heavy use for Christmas programs and events. It's been this way ever since the Great Hitching Post Brawl of Christmas Eve 1916. The Methodist reverend and the Catholic priest were both running late thanks to a snowstorm. The two duked it out over the last available carriage parking spot, and congregants from both churches jumped into the fray, landing all involved on the Naughty List. To avoid a repeat, the town manager strongly recommended that all holiday events be held at the chapel and open to the whole town. And that's the way it's been for over a hundred years.

"Okay. Do you have time to go there now?"

He glances at his watch and then his phone before answering. "Ariana texted to let me know she'll drop the Santa suit off at the inn. The girls have everything else under control. Let's do it."

I PULL into the cobblestone alley behind the chapel and park illegally. The Christmas in July crowds have arrived in force, and I feel some empathy for the long-ago men of the cloth and their parking woes. I wait in the car until Nick appears in my rearview mirror. He's moving fast, striding toward me from the direction of the library, where he returned Farah's car and checked in on Sage and Thyme.

When he reaches my back bumper, I open my door and step out into the alley. In the distance, I hear faint music, traffic noises, and voices raised in laughter.

"Ready?" he asks as I fall into step beside him.

"Ready."

I can't help swiveling around to confirm there's not a loser in a hat and sunglasses lurking in the bushes. Nick notices.

"I'm not going to let anything happen to you."

"I know."

I must not sound terribly convincing because he stops walking and turns to face me. I stop, too. His fingers are feather soft as he tips my chin up so that I'm staring into his eyes.

"Noe, I need you to hear this and believe it. I am *not* going to let anything happen to you." He rasps the words, his gold and brown starburst eyes searing my skin with their heat.

One hand slides down my arm coming to rest on my hip. The other circles the side of my neck, warm on my bare skin. He tugs me toward him and I move willingly, pressed up against him, my eyes still locked on his. My breath, hot and fast.

He dips his head, and my lips part, ready for his mouth on mine. More than ready.

And then he stops. He stops? He can't stop. There's no stopping in kissing. A mew of protest escapes my parted lips. He swallows.

"I'm going to kiss you now."

But he doesn't. Because I rise on my toes and kiss him first —softly, tentatively, sweetly.

A low rumble sounds in his throat and he yanks me even closer, my hips flush against his body, as he grips my neck and kisses me back. There's nothing soft, tentative, or sweet about it. He claims my mouth with his—hard, fast, and assured.

I arch my back and he digs his fingers into my hips. I'm twenty again. Transported by the familiar pressure of his mouth through time and space to a London street, oblivious to tutting passersby and honking cars. And at the same time, this kiss is nothing like any kiss we've shared. It's richer, deeper, and tinged with life and loss and need.

I don't think. I just give myself over to this feeling. And, wow, this feeling is strong. My ears ring. My chest vibrates with emotion. My ... eyes open and I tune into the fact that approximately four feet away and maybe ninety feet above us in the bell tower, the gigantic church bell is clanging.

The power of thought slowly returns to me, as the bell peals overhead. Oh, right. The bell. That's why we're here. I manage a shaky laugh and step back, pressing my hands flat against Nick's chest because I'm not quite ready to break contact.

"Church bell," I croak in response to his dazed expression.

He nods and drops his arm around my waist, snugging me

into his side. I lean in gratefully because my legs are jelly. We wait for the ringing to end and the bell to fall silent. It's a good thing we kissed. It's better than good—for many reasons, one of them being that it probably saved our hearing. If we hadn't detoured to explore one another's tonsils, we'd be up in the belfry right now.

Once I can hear myself think, I clear my throat. "So."

"So. Are we gonna talk about this now or after we look for the clue?" His eyes bore into mine. "Because make no mistake, Noelle, we *are* going to talk about it."

If I have anything to say about it, we're gonna do a lot more than *talk*. But I leave this thought unexpressed. "After. Let's get up in the tower and back down before the bell rings the half-hour."

He searches my face with a skeptical expression. "We are going to talk, though."

"Yes," I promise. "Come on, let's look for the clue."

I pull him toward the walkway that leads to the front of the white clapboard chapel. Together, we run up the three wide steps to the always-unlocked door and into the narthex.

Inside, the chapel is hushed, cool, and dimly lit. The sanctuary doors are propped open and the early evening sunlight streams through the high windows. As I peek in and see the altar at the front, I remember the last time I stood looking down the aisle. A sudden realization punches me in the chest.

"This is where you and Carol were married."

I know this, of course. I was her maid of honor. But the memory is a faded one. It wasn't front of mind when we decided to look here for the clue. I drop his hand, and he gives me a sidelong glance.

"What?"

So much for talking later. I take a breath and gesture toward the bench inside along the wall. "I have to tell you something before we look for the next clue."

He plants his feet. "You can tell me right here. We don't need to sit."

"Please?"

He pulls a face but parks his butt. I sit next to him and angle my knees toward him in a half-turn.

"So, what do you want to tell me?"

"How do I say this?"

"Just spit it out, Noelle. I'm a big boy. If you regret the kiss, I'll be—"

"—No!" I pull myself together and try again, less shouty. "I mean, no. I don't regret the kiss. I very much don't regret the kiss."

"Good." His mouth quirks into a satisfied grin. A very kissable grin.

"But," I continue before I get distracted by the extreme kissability of his lips, "remember when I told you Carol asked me to do something before she died?"

His grin evaporates. "Yes," he says carefully.

"She asked me if I still had feelings for you."

"She what?"

The only way out is through, I remind myself, paraphrasing Vermont's favorite poet. Then I blurt, "She said that she wanted us to be here for each other after she was gone."

He scrubs a hand over his face. "I don't understand."

"I don't know," I wail. "I hate that she died thinking I was lusting after her husband."

I don't know how I expect him to respond to this confession. But it's definitely not by laughing in my face. And yet, that's exactly what he does.

Unamused, I flop back against the bench, cross my arms, and wait for him to stop cracking up. Finally, he wipes his eyes with the back of his hand and takes a long breath.

"Sorry, Noelle. I can tell this has been eating at you."

"Well, yeah."

"Carol did *not* think you were lusting after me."

I give him the side-eye. "Hmph. Sure seems like it."

"How do I explain this?" He clicks his tongue against his teeth. "Okay, you know how some folks are really specific when they write their wills because they want to make sure their cherished possessions end up with people who truly appreciate their rock collection or first edition books or whatever?"

"I guess."

"That was Carol. At the end, she spent a lot of time trying to decide which of the girls would most love each piece of jewelry, which friend would want her sewing machine, who would take good care of her signed hockey puck. She chose something for everyone."

"This just confirms she was upset with me. She didn't choose anything for me."

The grin is back. "Yeah, she did. She gave you me." He stands up. "Come on. Let's go get the clue before the bell rings again."

I stare at his outstretched palm for a long moment. Then I take his hand and let him haul me to my feet and across the vestibule to a twisting flight of stairs.

CHAPTER 22

Nick

"How many more steps?" Noelle wonders aloud as we pass through the second-floor choir loft and take a shorter set of stairs to a small hallway.

"It can't be much further." I hope so, at least. The air up here is hot and stuffy.

At the end of the narrow corridor, there's a door set in the wall. Noelle opens it and pokes her head inside. From behind her, I can see a ladder to the next level.

She groans, and I give her a reminder. "It's better to keep moving. We don't want to be up there when the bell rings again."

She steps aside and ushers me forward. "Lead the way."

"Why do I feel like this is a ploy so you can look at my butt?"

"Because it is." She giggles.

I'm glad to see her laughing. She was so distressed when she sat me down on the bench. I couldn't imagine what she wanted to tell me. Definitely did not see 'your wife was trying to set us up from her deathbed' coming.

But, in retrospect, that's how Carol was. She probably saw something Noelle and I didn't. She was insightful that way. And she wasn't one to sit by and leave anything to chance—not when it came to the people she loved.

And she was right, wasn't she?

That kiss. That *kiss.* It wasn't *just* a kiss. The salty-sweet taste of her mouth, the soft curves of her body, her quiet sighs of pleasure—all of it familiar and new at the same time. Kissing Noelle was a homecoming and a revelation. And I want to get back to it as soon as humanly possible.

As if to taunt me, when I reach the top of the ladder and poke my head through the opening, I spot yet another ladder mounted on the opposite wall. "Frost me," I grumble as I pull myself up and turn around to offer Noelle a hand.

This level has small half-windows set low in the front wall. But we don't stop to admire the view. We clamber up the second ladder and finally reach the actual bell tower. This level is open, and the breeze is a welcome addition. Noelle boosts herself to her feet and stands beside me, lifting her tangle of copper-colored hair off her nape. I consider dropping a kiss on the smooth skin on the back of her neck.

But before I can engage in any delightful distractions, she pulls out the clue and frowns at it, then looks up at me all business.

"Tell me again. What does this Zuzu character say?"

I take a moment to replay the scene in my mind. The movie was one of Carol's favorites, so I've seen it dozens of times. But invariably one or more of the Jolly women is crying by the end, so sometimes Zuzu's line is drowned out by sobs or sniffles.

"She says, 'Teacher says every time a bell rings, an angel gets his wings.' That's the exact line of dialogue."

We both eye the bell. She tilts her head, thinking. "The clapper is the part that strikes the bell, right?"

"Right."

"So, that's what makes it ring."

She sticks her head inside the bell. So she's one of those. There are two kinds of people in this world—people who think nothing of sticking their hand down a garbage disposal to fish out an errant fork and people who turn off the power to the unit and flip the breaker for good measure before they retrieve the fork. I'm in the latter group, and she's making me antsy.

"Hurry up before you get *your* bell rung," I urge.

She laughs, and the sound echoes from inside the bell. But I'm not kidding. I'm just about to yank her out of there by force, when she ducks under the bell's rim and pops up beside me, waving a small envelope in triumph.

"It was attached to the swinging arm part."

"The axle?"

"Sure, why not?"

This envelope is labeled *Final Clue*. She tears it open and scans the note, her eyes racing over the words, and then passes it to me.

I read the typed phrase aloud, "'No space of regret can

make amends for one life's opportunity misused.' That doesn't sound like a clue, but it does sound familiar."

"It's a quote from Dickens' *A Christmas Carol*."

I hand it back to her. "I don't get it. It's labeled a clue, but how do we use it."

"Let's go get the map. Maybe it'll give us an idea."

We descend both ladders and both flights of stairs in silence. When we reach the narthex, she plops down on the bench.

"I thought you wanted to get the map."

"Shh, I'm thinking."

While she thinks, I study her face. I see the girl I loved in college in the curve of her cheek and the lift of her brow, and, of course, the glittering green of her eyes. But there's a new-to-me woman hidden under the smattering of freckles, too. I can't wait to get to know her.

"Hello? Earth to Nick. Did you hear me?" She's waving her hand in front of my face.

"Sorry, no I didn't. I was thinking about how gorgeous you are."

She turns pink. "Oh. That's an excellent excuse for tuning me out. Well done."

I laugh. "Can you repeat what you said?"

"Sure. Try not to be so dazzled by my beauty that you zone out again."

"I can't make any promises, but I'll try."

"What I said was the quote is from the beginning of the book, when Scrooge is visited by the ghost of his old business partner." She pauses meaningfully. "A guy named Jacob Marley."

"Huh, that's funny. Our family attorney is Marley Jacobs."

She nods. "I know. And her office is next door. That can't be a coincidence."

We race outside and across the alley to the Law Offices of Marley Jacobs. I scan the street for men in hats and sunglasses during the fifteen-second walk, but see no one.

As soon as we step inside the legal offices, I realize we have no plan.

Noelle looks around the minimalist waiting room. "There's no receptionist?"

I shake my head. "It's a paperless office. And I guess greeter-less, too. We always signed in on that tablet." I point out a tablet in a stand on a small white table. "But we always had an appointment."

"Well, if we guessed the clue correctly, she'll be expecting us—or me, at least." She shrugs and types her name in the box on the screen. Then she turns and tosses me a cellophane-wrapped chocolate peppermint candy from the bowl on the stand. "These are Merry's, right?"

"Yep." I unwrap it and pop it in my mouth, realizing it's the first thing I've eaten since the frittata at breakfast. "Do you want to grab an early dinner after this?"

She glances at the clock on the wall. "Sure."

We haven't even settled on the couch yet when the door to Marley's office opens, and she appears in the doorway. "Noelle?"

"Yes."

I'm about to insert myself into the conversation and explain our unusual request, but Marley turns her attention from Noelle to me and says, "Oh good, you came, too. You saved me a phone call. Come on back."

Noelle and I exchange a baffled look.

"Both of us?" she asks.

"Both of you," Marley tells her, holding the door open wide.

I follow Noelle through the open door, and Marley ushers us into her small conference room and tells us to make ourselves comfortable. We take seats at the same glass conference table where Carol and I signed our wills. I bounce my knee, uneasy and off-kilter.

A moment letter, Marley returns. She's holding a large rectangular box. Two thick envelopes rests on the lid. She deposits the box on the table directly in front of Noelle. Then she takes one of the two envelopes from the top and hands it to me. My name is printed on the front of it.

"Take as long as you need. I'd say if you have any questions, let me know. But the truth is, I don't know anything. I was asked to hold these items by a client."

"Can you tell us who the client is?" I ask, knowing it's a long shot.

"I suspect you'll be able to figure it out." Without further explanation, she steps out into the hall and pulls the door shut behind her.

After a long moment, Noelle clears her throat. "So, how should we do this? Open the envelopes at the same time? Take turns?"

"This is your scavenger hunt. You go first. Want to read them aloud?"

"Okay."

She rips the corner of the envelope's flap, slides her fingernail underneath, and tears it open. She removes a sheet of stationery. Unlike the clues, the letter is handwritten, not typed. She reads a few lines, then refolds it, and raises her eyes to meet mine.

"It's from Carol."

I'm speechless. I stare at the envelope in my hands. I'm holding a letter from my dead wife. I don't know how I'm supposed to feel. I don't know how I *do* feel.

After a beat, Noelle continues, "I don't think we should read these to each other. I'm sure yours will be very private."

I nod wordlessly and keep staring.

"Do you want me to open it for you?" she asks gently.

The question snaps me out of my frozen state. "No, thanks. I've got it."

"Okay." She reopens her letter and resumes reading.

I exhale and tear the envelope open like I'm a Neanderthal, tossing it on the table. The letter is written on a single page of thick paper in Carol's familiar looping script. I read it slowly, hearing her voice in my head as I do.

Darling Nick,

If all's gone according to plan, although I wrote this in August after I entered hospice, you're reading it in July, and I'm dead. Have been for a while. Oh, that hurts to write, so I can only imagine how much it hurts to live through.

When we learned I was dying, we agreed to leave nothing unsaid. It was important to me that you, Holly, Ivy, and Merry knew my heart and understood how much I love you all before I was gone. The conversations you and I are having now are, strangely, some of my favorites. There's something crystalizing about knowing you're dying, I suppose.

I kept one thing from you, though. I'm sorry.

I didn't think you were ready to hear it then. I hope you are now. When I told you I hoped you'd find a new partner one day, someone to share the rest of your life with, I meant it. But I actually have someone in mind for you: Noelle.

I know both of you better than anyone else on this planet, and I know in my cancerous bones that you'll be good together. Not better than you and me, because we were pretty dang amazing. But good in a different way, a beautiful way. I could lay out all the reasons you two belong together, but won't it be more fun to figure it out yourself?

Now if you've already met someone, this is awkward. Also, wow, didn't let the grass grow underfoot, huh? Just kidding. If you have met someone or you think I'm wrong, ignore me. It's not like I can do anything to convince you. Unless I decide to haunt you, I guess.

Where was I? Oh, right. I know I'm right about you and Noelle. Not because you had a short relationship more than a quarter century ago, but because of the people you both are now. You're my two favorite humans (who I did not give birth to) and I hate to leave you behind. But if you take care of each other, I'll feel better about it.

By the way, I tried to talk to Noelle about this and she freaked out. That's when I got the idea to create a scavenger hunt for her. My hope is she found her way to the truth along with the clues. And I hope you have, too.

You have to live for both of us now, Nick. And I want you to love.

Always yours, that'll never change,
Carol

P.S.—Please thank Griselda. She did all the legwork for me because I couldn't exactly run all over town.

I close the letter and try to swallow around the lump in my throat. Across the table, tears run down Noelle's cheeks.

CHAPTER 23

Noelle

My cheeks are wet. I wipe away my tears with a shaking hand, take a shuddering breath, and read Carol's letter for a second time.

Noelle, ma belle,

I'm so sorry. Sorry that I'm dead and I can't tell you this in person. And sorry that I upset you by asking if you have feelings for Nick.

You do, you know. Well, you don't know, now, when I'm writing this. But maybe by the time you read this, you'll have clued in. In case you haven't, allow me to point it out: You and Nick have a connection. This isn't about your college romance. Or maybe, in part, it is. But you share more than that. You share ME, you doofus.

Don't you see that if you're together, it's not a betrayal of me or what Nick and I had? It's the opposite. Through your love for each other, you'll keep my love and my light alive.

*Am I saying that if you don't get with Mistletoe Mountain's most eligible widower, really, **you'll** have killed me, not the cancer? Yes. No, just kidding. But I am saying that you and Nick belong together. I tried to guide you to this realization through the scavenger hunt. Did it work? And was it fun?*

I had fun coming up with the clues for you. It brought back so many memories of so many Christmases in July, of us when we were girls (I'd forgotten all about the letterboxing fad!), of taking my girls to the festivals together. Of so much.

I wish we could have elevenses again. I'd give anything to sit with you in my kitchen, drinking tea, gabbing, and laughing until our sides hurt. But we can't, and that sucks eggnog.

That's what your last clue is about. When the ghost of Jacob Marley warns Scrooge that "no space of regret can make amends for one life's opportunity misused," you know what he's saying, right? When you get to the end, Noelle, you don't want to have regret for chances you didn't take. Believe me, as much as I hate that I'm dying, I don't have regrets. I know I used my time on this earth the way I wanted to.

*I want you to have this same certainty someday (in the distant, distant future). You used to seize every opportunity, take every chance, and chase every dream. You moved to **two** different countries, alone. You started a masters' program in a language you don't speak! That Noelle would not be scared to open her heart—especially not to someone who will take the care with it that Nick will.*

Let him in. For me. If it doesn't work out (which it totally will), move on, and let someone else in.

Don't make me drag myself around your cottage in chains moaning at you like you're Ebenezer Scrooge. I have better things to do in my afterlife.

Love,
Carol

At some point during my second read-through, my tears turn to laughter. It's as if Carol is sitting across from me, eating scones and telling me how it is. And my heart, which was so heavy, is light. Full, but light.

I look up to see Nick watching me.

"You okay?" His voice is husky.

I nod. "I am. Are you?"

"I'm good. Carol, she's something else."

A smile blooms on my lips. "Yes, she is."

He jerks his chin. "What's in the box? Did the letter say?"

I blink. "No, it didn't."

I forgot all about the box. I stand up, pull it toward me,

and remove the lid. Several sheets of green tissue paper are wrapped around the contents of the box. I unfold the thin paper and lift out a red, short-sleeved, A-line vintage cocktail dress with a white shawl collar and two rows of white buttons on the bodice. I hold it up and meet Nick's eye.

"This is Carol's summer Mrs. Claus dress," I say slowly.

"I think it's yours now. If you want it."

Mine?

I blink and break eye contact. I look down at the dress in my hands and spot a note tucked into one of the pockets. I pluck it out and read it aloud.

*Noelle, Nick's going to need a Mrs. Claus for the Christmas
in July festival. It's easy: wear the dress, smile at the kids,
and hand out the candy canes. ~ Carol*

He guffaws. Then his face grows serious. He pushes back his chair and stands up, facing me. "Will you do it?"

Dickens' admonition—and Carol's—runs through my mind. I almost have to, don't I? Take this chance, seize this opportunity?

"If the dress fits, I'll do it," I say.

He grins widely. Without thinking, I stretch up on my tiptoes and drop a kiss on the corner of his upper lip. He takes the dress from me, gently returns it to the box, and covers my mouth with deep, searching kisses.

More kissing? I could get used to this. I picture a life where there's just so much kissing. Kissing over breakfast frittatas, at red lights, while walking a dog that we don't have but could get, during fiercely competitive Scrabble games that I will obviously win. My mind spins out a future while my mouth responds eagerly to Nick's need. I wrap my arms around his neck and lace my fingers together behind his head.

He comes up for air. "Carol was right."

I give him a look. "Duh. Carol was *always* right."

He laughs, then dives back into his thorough exploration of my mouth. I pull him closer. He can't be close enough to satisfy me. As his tongue dances with mine, his hands skim my waist, and then he brushes his fingers across the sliver of bare skin between the top of my yoga pants and the hem of my shirt. A delicious shiver runs through me.

He growls low in his throat and moves his lips to my neck. I press into him and—

The door flies open. "Noelle? Is that your blue hatchback parked in the alley?"

Marley Jacobs peers at us with a mixture of curiosity, amusement, and concern as we jump apart.

I smooth my hair and straighten my shirt. "Yeah. I know it's parked illegally. We're done here, I think, so I'll   "

She holds up a hand. "I just caught someone breaking into it."

MY PASSENGER SIDE window is smashed in. Glass covers the seat and the console. While I survey the damage, Marley and Nick stand a few feet away near the rear door of her office building, arguing in hushed tones over whether they should call the police.

"It's the first night of Summer Christmas," Marley is

saying. "Yes, of course, report it. She'll probably have to for her insurance, anyway. But the cops are going to have their hands full with visitors succumbing to elevation sickness and driving their expensive cars into dry creek beds because our road signs were designed as some sort of inside joke. Besides, I didn't get a good look at the guy's face before he ran off." I know what's coming next before she says it. "And he was wearing a baseball cap and sunglasses. I wouldn't be able to pick him out of a crowd, let alone a lineup."

Nick mutters a response that includes the word 'stalker' while I try to breathe. I'm suddenly hot and dizzy. I lean forward, grabbing the window frame to steady myself.

"Hey, careful, you're gonna cut yourself." Nick sprints to me and gently moves me back a step. "Besides, there might be fingerprints. You shouldn't touch."

At least I think that's what he says. It's hard to hear him through the buzzing in my ears. I sway in his arms.

"Light-headed … eat something … dizzy, hot …." I'm trying hard to make sense and full sentences, but I can't.

Marley springs into action and runs up beside us. "Give me your keys."

I reach my shaky hand into my pocket, dig out the keys, and drop them into her palm.

"I'll pull it into my lot. Nick, take her inside. There's a jug of apple cider in my kitchenette. She probably has low blood sugar and the shock and stress are making it worse. Noelle, you drink some cider. Sip it slowly. Go."

Nick scoops me up, and I interlace my fingers behind his neck and let my head loll back against his chest. He carries me in his arms as he runs for the door. It would be romantic if I weren't somehow simultaneously sweating and shivering. He kicks the door open with his foot and deposits me on the couch in Marley's waiting room. There's a light blanket folded neatly over the back of the sofa, and he drapes it over my shoulders.

"I'm going to get the cider. Don't move." He drops a kiss on the crown of my head and runs toward the back of the office.

As promised, he's right back. He presses a coffee mug that reads 'A Good Lawyer Knows the Law, A Great Lawyer Knows the Judge' into my hands.

"Take a sip," he urges, crouching in front of me and watching me with worried eyes.

I raise the mug to my lips and let the cold, crisp sweetness run down my throat. He reaches for the mug and rests it on the side table. "That's enough for now."

I nod and swallow. "Thank you."

He shakes his head. "Don't you thank me. I'm going to spend the rest of my life taking care of you."

I manage a weak laugh. "Carol's letter said *I'm* supposed to take care of *you.*"

He grins and the skin around his eyes crinkles sexily. "I guess we'll have to take care of each other then."

I swear I could swim in his hazel eyes. I reach for the cider and take another small drink.

"I'm starting to feel human again," I tell him.

He opens his mouth to answer just as Marley bangs through her own front door, eyes blazing. She locks the door. Then she pulls the shades over the window in the door and the big glass window behind the couch.

I give Nick a wide-eyed look. He shakes his head. Of

course, he doesn't know anything more than I do. But his mouth is a firm, hard line.

Marley cocks her head and gives me a close look. "The color's back in your face. Good. Let's go to my office."

She carries the mug of cider and Nick insists on carrying me, even though I'm sure I can walk without any problem at this point. But if the man wants to carry me around like I'm Cleopatra, who am I to argue?

Once we're all settled in Marley's light, airy office, she wastes no time. She slaps a sheet of paper on the desk. "This was in the footwell wrapped around a rock. Presumably, the rock used to smash the window."

I stare down at the angry, scrawled words, and my heart palpitates. My mouth goes dry and my throat tightens. This is my worst nightmare, a nightmare that's dogged me for twenty-seven years, and it's come to life. I reach for the cider and take a long gulp.

Nick frowns at the message. "What does *ti ucciderò, puttana* mean?" he asks, butchering the Italian.

Marley gives me another piercing look. "It's a threat."

I clear my throat and choke out an answer, "Literally translated, it means 'I will kill you, whore.'"

My words hang on the air, heavy and malevolent.

Then Nick growls, "This isn't just some creep messing with your scavenger hunt. Clearly, this guy is disturbed and possibly dangerous."

Marley nods. "My thinking about involving the authorities has evolved." She stops herself, then goes on, "That's lawyer for I was wrong. You need to call the cops. And I'll reach out to the District Attorney's Office."

"No DA," I say instantly.

She frowns. "You're aware Nick's daughter works for the DA, right?"

"Right, and that's why we're not involving the DA. I don't want Holly anywhere near this guy. We can call the sheriff, for all the good it'll do. But no DA."

Something about my tone tips Nick off. "You just figured out who it is, didn't you?"

I nod, staring at the note. I take a shaky breath, then another. When I trust myself to speak, I say, "I did. His name is Dante Bianchi. And I don't know how he found me." I jab my finger down on the paper. "But this isn't an idle threat. He means it."

CHAPTER 24

Nick

*D*ante *Bianchi.* My blood boils as the name loops through my brain. I clench my hands into fists then relax them—fist, release, fist, release—while Marley guides us through a phone interview with a frazzled sheriff's deputy. Deputy Wells promises to run Bianchi's name through the system and makes some noises about having a patrol car drive down Poinsettia Way a few times during the night.

I lean toward the octopus-shaped speaker phone and enunciate. "She's not going back to her cottage."

Noelle raises an eyebrow. "I'm not?"

"No. Absolutely not. You're coming back to the inn."

"Probably best," the deputy's crackly voice agrees from the speaker. "More people around."

"Too many people around," Noelle argues. "The place is

fully booked, and you have three extra people in your private space already. There's no room for me at the inn."

"Well, you're not sleeping in a manger. And you're not going back to the cottage. So we'll figure it out."

Noelle frowns. Too bad. She's coming home with me, and that's that.

Marley taps her silver pen on her notepad and scans her notes. Then she ticks items off on her fingers, "The Snowflake Cafe, the woods behind Snow Lake, Alpine Jewelers, the library, Dancing Ladies, and the alley behind the chapel. Is that everything? All the times this Bianchi person popped up."

"I think so," Noelle says.

I snap my fingers. "The ski lodge! Enrique was walking his dog yesterday morning and saw that someone had broken in. It looks like they were sleeping there. Smashed a window to get in. We boarded it up, and Enrique said he'd call county park and recreation to let them know."

"Noelle wasn't there, right?" Deputy Wells asks.

"No, but he has to be sleeping somewhere."

"I'll add it to the report," she says doubtfully. "But it could have been teenagers. And if it was your guy, once he sees the window's been boarded up, he won't go back."

"How's he getting around?" Marley asks. "He can't be on foot. The strip club and the lodge are miles outside of town in opposite directions."

"I'll reach out to the car rental agencies at the airports. He probably flew through JFK and then to Burlington." Then the deputy groans. "Unless he was smart enough to fly into Montreal, rent a car there, and drive across the border. If he did that, it's gonna be much harder to track him."

Noelle gulps. "He's very smart," she says in a flat voice.

"In that case, keep your head on a swivel," Wells advises. "I'll be in touch as soon as I know something."

"Thank you, deputy." Marley ends the call and studies us. "I don't like this one bit."

"That makes two of us," I tell her.

"Three," Noelle whispers.

"Do you need me to drive you to the inn? You shouldn't walk," Marley points out.

"Thanks, but I already called the inn. Ivy's on her way to pick us up. You've done plenty."

"Yes, thank you," Noelle says.

Marley waves off the gratitude. "Of course. I just wish I'd been faster. If I could have caught the guy, this would all be over."

Noelle widens her eyes. "Marley, listen to me, this guy is *very* dangerous. If you see him again, don't try to be a hero. Sensei Adam's training isn't a match for him. Do you understand?"

Marley must clock the terror in Noelle's face the same as I do. She answers in a grim tone, "Noted."

WE STAND INSIDE BEHIND LOCKED door and watch the street for Ivy's beat-up Volvo wagon. When she pulls up in front of the building, Marley unlocks the door and we run to the car. Noelle's hugging the dress box to her chest like it's an infant. I yank the back passenger side door open and hustle her and her box into the car, then race around to the other side of the car and slide in next to her.

Ivy waits until we're buckled in to pull out. "We're going to take the scenic route. The square is teeming with revelers."

"Got it."

Rosemary twists around from the passenger seat. "Ivy filled me in, so I called my husband. No shade to your local authorities, but Dave knows some people from a previous investigation. Thyme's sister-in-law was being stalked by her ex-husband. It was an international thing because the ex was calling the shots from Brazil. Dave's going to reach out to his contacts about this Dante Bianchi."

"Thank you," Noelle whispers, wringing her hands in her lap.

I reach over and cover Noelle's hand with mine while I thank my niece. "I appreciate this, Rosemary."

"Of course." She hesitates, then says, "Mom wanted me to let you know you're both welcome at Tranquility. He won't think to look for you in New Jersey."

For the first time in years, I feel grateful for my meddling sister. "That's not a bad idea—"

Beside me, Noelle snaps up straight and says in a steely voice, "No. I'm done running. And your uncle is playing Santa this weekend."

Rosemary studies her determined face for a moment. "Okay, I get it. The offer stands, though."

Ivy pipes up, "Dad, I know you want Noelle to stay away from her cottage, but she might want to pick up some clothes or toiletries. Rosemary and I can run in and get her a few things."

"No. Absolutely not. Nobody's going near Noelle's house. Surely between the six of you, you can lend her anything she needs." It's out of the question.

Ivy nods. "Understood. We set up the guest cottage in the backyard for Noelle. It's more private."

"I thought your cousins were staying there?" Noelle worries.

"We decided to double up in our old bedrooms. Rosemary and Holly, Sage and me, and Merry and Thyme. It'll be fun. Like a sleepover."

Only Ivy still lives at the inn. Holly and Merry have their own places in town. But during the holidays, they stay in their girlhood bedrooms in our private wing. In part, to help with the guests, and, in part, because it's a tradition. Getting the guest house ready for Noelle is a sweet gesture, and I'm sure she'll appreciate the privacy. But there's no way she's staying there alone. I'm not letting her out of my sight until Dante Bianchi is behind bars or in the ground.

MY DAUGHTERS, with the help of their cousins, have outdone themselves. When Ivy pulls up in front of the inn, Noelle gasps. The wide, graceful porch is festooned with twinkling lights and hanging baskets bursting with red-and-white striped petunias. Two large wreaths of silver jingle bells decorate the double doors.

"The place looks great," I say as Ivy pulls into the driveway.

She meets my eye in the rearview mirror and grins. "We had fun doing it." She follows the long driveway past our guest parking area and brings the wagon to a stop in front of the cottage. "Merry had her homemade baked macaroni and cheese in the oven when we left. We can bring some out for you and Noelle."

Smart kid. My daughter knows I'm not leaving Noelle alone in the guest house. Before I can say that sounds great, Noelle clears her throat.

"It's the night before Christmas in July. You always have your family dinner tonight, before the chaos starts. I'm not depriving you of that. Not this year. We'll come eat with you. Just give me time to take a shower. It's been a long day."

My heart threatens to explode in my chest. After the wild emotional roller coaster she's been on today, Noelle's main concern is for my daughters and their first Christmas in July without their mother.

A small smile plays over Ivy's lips. "That sounds awesome. We'll get some clean clothes together for you and bring them out. Is dinner at seven okay?"

"Seven's perfect," Noelle tells her.

I help her out of the car with the unwieldy box and hustle to the front door of the tiny cottage. Ivy waits until I've punched in the code and unlocked the front door to pull out and drive behind the guesthouse to the garage where we park our personal vehicles.

I usher Noelle into the sparkling cottage. It's been cleaned from top to bottom and a giant Minerva amaryllis in a silver pot graces the small kitchen island, its red tipped petals and white star center adding a playful holiday touch. She smiles and runs a finger over a petal.

"I haven't been out here in years. I forgot how cute it is."

"Well, you're in for a treat. We remodeled the bathroom, and the shower is a masterpiece. So take off your clothes and enjoy yourself. I mean—"

She cuts me off with a kiss. "I know what you meant. And I will."

I laugh then grow serious. "But after your shower, before dinner, you're going to tell me what happened with Dante Bianchi."

Her green eyes are somber as she nods. "I will."

She heads for the bathroom and I pace around the small cottage like a tiger prowling in his cage. While the water runs in the next room, Holly brings over some clothes for Noelle and then I make a list of people who I trust. It's a long list, and I'm glad for that.

The water shuts off. A minute later, Noelle emerges from the bathroom. She has a towel wrapped around her hair and another, larger one, covers her body. Through sheer willpower, I ignore my body's reaction to her standing, practically naked, mere feet away from me.

"There's a bag of clothes on the bed," I croak.

"Thanks," she chirps, then disappears.

The image of her dropping her towel fills my head, and I drive it out with an alphabetical list of resorts. I'm at M for Mandarin Oriental when she reappears in the living area. Her damp hair is piled up on top of her head in a mess of red curls and she's wearing a soft-looking pale purple, long-sleeved top and a pair of faded jeans that hug her curves. Her face is bare of makeup and slightly flushed from the hot shower. She looks vulnerable, young, and so freaking scared.

"Feel better?" I ask around the lump in my throat.

"Much."

She crosses the room and curls up in the corner of the small loveseat with her feet tucked up beneath her. She pats the cushion, and I join her, turning sideways on the other end of the divan so we're facing each other. Even from here, she smells like lemons and vanilla.

"Dante Bianchi," I prompt.

She closes her eyes for a moment, and her long lashes brush her cheeks. Then she takes a breath, opens her eyes, and catches her lower lip between her teeth. After a moment, she starts talking.

"Let me get this whole story out without interruption, okay?"

"I'll hold my questions till the end," I tell her wryly.

She smirks. "Wiseacre." Then her expression changes. "Dante Bianchi was my master's program advisor. He was also, coincidentally, my supervisor for the research position I had the summer before the program was supposed to start. At first, he was fine. Charming, even. He flirted with me, but I didn't think anything of it. For one thing, it was Italy. I think the men are required by law to flirt with any woman who has a pulse. And for another, he was in a position of authority over me. The university's code of conduct was clear about the boundaries for relationships—and that would have been out of bounds."

She's about a minute into this story, and I'm already breaking my promise not to interrupt. "If it hadn't been, would you have been interested? I'm not jealous," I assure her. "Just trying to get the full picture."

She considers the question for a moment, pursing her lips,

then shakes her head. "No. He was a little too intense for my tastes. And I really was laser-focused on getting my master's. I wasn't looking for a relationship or even a fling."

"Got it. I'll try not to interrupt again."

She nods and picks up the thread of her story again. "As the summer went on, the flirting turned into something more like harassment. He'd pinch my butt when I walked by. Made a lot of comments about my body. Just gross stuff. I told myself to ignore it, but he was relentless. And while I could put up with it for the summer, there was no way I wanted to deal with him on the regular for two more years once the program started."

I clench my fists and dig my fingers into my palms but manage to keep my mouth shut. She pauses to take a deep breath. Her pulse is visible in her throat.

"So I made my first mistake. I went to the international students' office and asked for help switching my advisor. I told them why, thinking it would be kept confidential. They agreed to assign a new advisor, but they told Dante what I'd said."

"That's on them, not you," I tell her roughly.

She gives me a look. "Try harder not to interrupt or I'll never get it out."

I clamp my jaw closed.

"Dante was livid. The next day, he came into the archives and cornered me. He pushed me against the wall, got right in my face, and spat on me. He warned me that I wouldn't like what happened if I said another negative word about him. I was freaking out. I realized I wasn't going to survive two years in a small program with this guy whether he was my advisor or not. He had it out for me after that, professionally. But he was also infatuated or obsessed or something. He told people we were dating. And I was afraid to correct him, you know?"

I nod my understanding and manage not to say anything.

"By the time I got Carol's letter asking me to be her maid of honor, I'd already decided to drop out of the program. I figured I'd come home for your wedding, regroup, and then get my master's in London or somewhere here. The University of Washington in Seattle has a great program, and I knew people there."

She pauses and clears her throat. Her gaze drops to her lap. Pain radiates off her in waves. I can't take it, so I pull her toward me and wrap an arm around her shoulder, stroking her damp hair with my other hand.

She fills her lungs with air and continues. "I didn't tell anyone my plan. I knew it would set him off.

But I started packing. What I didn't know was that he'd been spying on me. When he saw the boxes through my bedroom window, he broke into my apartment and … uh … pleasured himself all over my comforter."

I snarl, and she presses her palm against my chest. "Please just let me get this out. I freaked. I called the police, which was my second mistake. They completely blew me off. They said there was no proof it was him." She raises her head to look at me with tears shining in her eyes. "The one officer told me I should be *flattered*. That it was a compliment."

I'm seconds away from exploding, but I hold it together.

She goes on, "Then it got worse. I don't know how he did it, but after that, Dante somehow got his hands on my passport. I was keeping it on me at all times. But one afternoon, I opened my bag and it was missing from the zippered pocket where I'd been keeping it. In its place, there was a note: *ti ucciderò, puttana.* I'll kill you, whore. I knew it was him, and I knew nobody would believe me. He was very popular in the department, and I was some random American. I've never been so scared in my life."

Her shoulders shake, and I rub her back and make soothing noises while she sobs. After a minute, she wipes her tears and says, "I was in the ladies' room having what I now know was a panic attack. The door opened and this woman, Marta, walked in. She was another international graduate student, from Poland. Her English wasn't great, and my Polish is nonexistent. The handful of times we did speak, it was in Italian, so I didn't really know her. But she saved my life. I was sitting on the floor with my back against the wall, hyperventilating. She didn't even look at me. She crouched beside me and placed my passport on the floor. Then, washed her hands, and walked out of the bathroom without saying a word."

Her heart is thumping wildly. I can feel it against my chest.

"I opened the window and crawled out onto the ledge. Thank heavens I was only on the second floor. I jumped to the ground, walked to the train station and caught the first train to the airport. Then I emptied my bank account and bought a one-way ticket home leaving the next day. I slept in the terminal. Tried to sleep, anyway. I was still half-convinced Dante would find me and drag me back to Ravenna. But he didn't. I came home and never left. The end."

She pulls herself up and gives me a crooked smile. "Any questions."

"Just one. How can you think any of this is your fault?"

She shakes her head. "I handled it all wrong. I didn't understand how disturbed he was, how much danger I was in. I should have—"

I press my finger against her parted lips to still them. "No. I'm not going to let you blame yourself for any bit of this. It kills me that you've spent twenty-plus years beating yourself up over this piece of human garbage. Not one minute more, do you understand?"

She stares at me for a moment. Then she nods, and those green eyes fill again. I thumb a tear away from her eye and drop a gentle kiss in its place.

"You're safe now, Noelle. This isn't Ravenna. This is Mistletoe Mountain, and Dante Bianchi's about to learn the difference."

CHAPTER 25

Noelle

I expect to be wrung out and tired after telling Nick the whole miserable story about Dante, but to my surprise, it's the opposite. Sharing my shameful secret feels like slipping off a heavy backpack after a long hike. I feel lighter and freer. I am exhausted, though. Also, ravenous and ready to shovel mac-and-cheese into my face with wild abandon.

As we walk from the guest cottage to the main house, Nick grabs my hand. I lace my fingers through his and take a deep breath to inhale the sweet jumble of scents from the flower garden. The fire pit and patio are aglow under string lights, and fireflies wink off and on in the trees. Clusters of guests mill around with beers and cocktails. Nick greets everyone in our path with a cheerful word and a handshake. He remembers names and hometowns, and several regulars offer him hugs and condolences. I can feel their curiosity as they look me over, but Nick makes no move to introduce me, and, for that, I'm grateful. Let them wonder. I just want to *eat.*

When we walk into the kitchen, I expect him to drop my hand, but he pulls me closer. I give him a sidelong look.

"You're not planning to tell your daughters we're … whatever we are … tonight, are you?" I whisper.

"Why not? They're adults."

"It's a family holiday," I counter.

"You're basically family," he shoots back.

"We don't even know what we *are,*" I point out. "And there's the small matter of the guy running around town threatening to kill me. Maybe this announcement could wait until, say, next week?"

"Nah."

I'm about to argue further, when Merry bustles into the room and shoos us into the family dining room. The table is set, wine and water are poured, and the biggest casserole dish I've ever seen rests on a tile tray, steam rising from a perfectly browned mountain of macaroni and cheese. An even bigger salad bowl holds a green salad.

"Sit," Merry instructs taking the chair that used to be her mom's—the one closest to the kitchen, in case she needed to run out to check on a dish.

The others have left two chairs together at the far end of the table. Nick pulls one out for me, and I sit down next to Sage. He takes the chair on the end and reaches for my hand under the table.

"Everything looks delicious," I tell Merry.

She beams. "Let's dig in."

We pass the dishes family-style. Once everyone has a mound of mac-and-cheese and a salad, Nick raises his wine glass.

"Thank you to my amazing daughters for taking charge of the open house. You were right, and I was wrong to want to cancel. And thank you to the best nieces a guy could ask for. You three came through for us, and that means a lot."

They chorus 'hear, hear' and clink glasses.

When the table falls silent, I clear my throat. "I also want to thank you for letting me crash your party."

Holly turns to me, dead serious, and says, "Crash the party? Aren't you our new mom?"

I gape at her.

After a moment, she burst out laughing. "I'm kidding, Noelle. Oh, you should have seen your face."

"Stop it," her father admonishes her through his own laughter. Then he clears his throat. "But you might as well know, Noelle and I are …" He throws me a look. "Dating?"

"Sure. Dating."

"Duh."

I look at Ivy. "Duh?"

She nods. "It might not have been obvious to you two, but to anyone with a brain, this was inevitable."

Her sisters nod vigorously.

Thyme interjects, "I mean, we've only been here since Tuesday, and *we* knew."

Oh.

"We're all happy for you—for both of you," Merry assures me. "Now, eat before the food gets cold."

"Don't have to ask me twice," I tell her, digging in.

The meal passes quickly. We go around the table saying three things. Mine are that I'm grateful for their kindness and love (squeezing Nick's hand under the table as I say this), I regret that I didn't put the pieces together about Dante sooner, and I'm going to get a good night's sleep so I can be helpful at the open house tomorrow.

When the food is gone, and everyone has ruefully agreed we're too full for one of Merry's desserts, Nick says, "A quick word about tomorrow before you all scatter."

They fall silent and turn to their dad.

"We want our guests to have a memorable, wonderful experience, like always. But we need to be alert. Dante Bianchi is a threat to Noelle. We have to take that seriously. So if you see anyone or anything that looks out of place, let me know right away. Understand?"

They nod in unison.

Rosemary holds up a finger.

"Yes?"

"Dave called me right before dinner. He said Bianchi has an active European Arrest Warrant in the system for kidnapping. So, basically, the entire Western Hemisphere is under a BOLO notice on him."

"BOLO?" Merry asks.

"Be on the lookout," several people explain at once.

"That's good, right?" she wants to know.

"It can't be bad," Rosemary tells her.

"Thanks for getting that information," Nick says. "I'll pass it along to Deputy Wells."

She wrinkles her nose. "Dave already did. Hope you

don't mind. He said the sheriff's department might take it more seriously coming from another law enforcement officer."

"Of course we don't mind. Thank you, and thank him for me," I say. I finish my wine and shake my head. "I'm not surprised he has a criminal record. But I *am* surprised he turned up here. I can't imagine how he found me."

"I can," Sage says.

We turn to look at her.

"You can?"

"Yeah. That article in the library lobby about the children's wing said you garnered international industry attention for the design and the program. If he's still in library sciences or whatever, he probably saw it."

My heart skips a beat. Of course. And *The Journal of Library Innovation* ran a long, glowing piece, complete with a stupid picture of my stupid face.

"I'm sure that's it," I tell her. "I got careless."

Nick lowers his chin and gives me a 'you've got to be kidding' look. "You didn't get careless. You were living your life. There was no reason to think some creep would see the article and travel across the globe to terrorize you."

He's right. Intellectually, I know he's right. But I can't help feeling like I brought this on myself.

Rosemary leans across the table. "Hey, not to change the subject. But what was that box you had when we picked you up? Did you finish the scavenger hunt?"

"Oh, I didn't tell you. Yes, we did." I smile at Nick.

"Dad helped?" Ivy asks.

"He did."

"Well, what was the surprise? And did you figure out who set it up?"

I look at Nick. This is his story as much as mine.

He refills his wineglass and says, "Your mother did, last August. Apparently, she got Griselda to hide the clues for her."

"That's just like Mom," Merry says.

"The surprise was two things," I tell them. "Your mom's Mrs. Claus dress was in the box along with a note asking me to play the role this weekend."

Ivy claps her hands together and squeals. "You're gonna do it, right?"

I nod. "I am."

"Yesssss."

"What was the second surprise?" Thyme wants to know.

"Carol wrote me a letter. She wrote one for Nick, too. I don't know exactly what his says, but, um, she wanted me to know it would make her happy if your father and I ... dated."

"In broad strokes, that's what my letter said, too," Nick confirms.

Holly shakes her head and says fondly, "Isn't that just like Mom? She's a control freak even from beyond the grave."

Just then, her watch beeps. She glances down at the time, then jumps to her feet. "It's T minus eighteen hours until the open house, people! Does everyone have their assignments? Any questions?"

Loud laughter drowns out the rest of her instructions.

She turns to me with a confused expression. "What's so funny?"

I give her a gentle smile. "I think it's that you're the living embodiment of the expression the apple doesn't fall far from the tree."

CHAPTER 26

Nick
Friday

I wake early with a stiff neck from sleeping on the too-short couch, a smile when I remember that Noelle's just feet away in the bedroom, and a to-do list as long as Santa's beard. I stretch lazily and decide I should bring Noelle coffee in bed to start her day. I scratch my belly and glance at the bedroom door. It's ajar.

I launch myself off the couch and bolt toward the bedroom. That door was closed all night. There's no way Bianchi got in here right under my nose. I burst into the room, ready for anything.

Anything, that is, except what I find. Noelle stands in front of the antique mirror in the corner, pirouetting in the Mrs. Santa sundress or whatever it is. I think she called it a cocktail dress. Aptly named, because the sight of her in it has my co—never mind.

She catches my eye in the mirror, and I cover the front of my boxers with both hands.

"Morning."

"Uh, yeah, morning."

"I'm just trying on the dress."

"I see that." I cough. "It looks like it was made for you."

She beams. Then her eyes travel down my bare chest and further south. She bursts into laughter. I try not to take offense.

"Sorry," she says after she catches her breath. "Your boxers are cute."

I look down at the surfing Santas that festoon my underwear. "Oh, right. You might as well know, I always wear Christmas boxers."

She raises an eyebrow. "Not *always*, right?"

"I counted once. I have forty-seven pairs of Christmas themed boxer shorts. So, yep. Always."

"You're a very dedicated St. Nick," she tells me as she walks toward me.

When she's about six inches away, I swallow hard. "I'm warning you now, Noe. If you come any closer, we're going to run behind Holly's timetable all day because I'm *this close* to ripping that dress off you and taking you to bed."

Her chest rises in the snug bodice and a pink stain colors her cheeks. Her lips part. "Oh."

We stare at each other for a long, long moment. I can feel the heat rising off her body. My pulse rushes. Finally, I grit my teeth and say, "I'm gonna put some clothes on and get the coffee started."

Her eyes are still locked on mine, heavy with desire, but she nods. "Good idea. We have a big day. I'll get dressed and meet you in the kitchen."

I turn and take my surfing Santa-covered butt out of the room before my willpower deserts me.

Ten minutes later, we're fully dressed, drinking coffee at the butcher block kitchen island, and splitting one of the Jule-logs that Merry left in the fridge.

"Nothing like a healthy breakfast of caffeine and chocolate," Noelle observes.

"It's an occupational hazard, Mrs. Claus. For the next three days, you'll be running on pure sugar."

She wrinkles her nose. "Oh, that's unfortunate."

"Next week is all about vegetables, clean proteins, and gallons of water to even it out."

"Fair enough." She pops another morsel of chocolate sponge into her mouth.

"That's the spirit. Last night, you said you would help with open house. What about the library?"

"We close for the duration of the Christmas in July festival and let the performers use our parking lot."

"Didn't know. I always walk over to the gazebo."

"In any event, I'm all yours."

"I like the sound of that." I lean over and nuzzle her neck.

She drops the cake and crawls into my lap. We're making out like a pair of teenagers, when there's a knock at the door.

I ease her to the floor and open the door to see Thyme standing on the little porch, wide-eyed.

"Morning, Thyme."

"Good morning, Uncle Nick. Hi, Noelle." She gives me an apologetic smile. "Holly wants to know whether you plan to join us or if you're going to slack off all day."

I glance at my watch. "It's not even six-thirty yet."

"Correct. But if you check the timetable, you'll see that work assignments started at six o'clock."

We stare at each other for a moment.

"What have I done?"

"It appears you created a monster, Uncle Nick. Rosemary is intense, but she has nothing on Holly."

Noelle places a hand on my arm. "I'll talk to her. She's probably overcompensating because she's afraid she won't live up to Carol's precedent."

As soon as she says it, I know she's right. My Grinchy heart grows at least one size as I think of the impossible task Holly's set for herself. "No, I'll do it. She needs to hear it from me that she's doesn't have to compete with her mom. She can put her own stamp on the open house."

She smiles. "That'll mean a lot to her."

I give her a quick, chaste kiss, then turn to Thyme. "Please wait for Noelle so you can walk over to the inn together. I don't want you to be alone. I'll clear things up with the boss."

Noelle protests. "It's broad daylight. And it's only seventy yards."

I remember the icy fist of fear that gripped me when I saw the bedroom door hanging open and repeat myself. "And I don't want you to be alone. Not even to walk across the property. Not until Bianchi's off the street."

She turns her mouth down, but nods.

"Tell me you understand."

"I understand," she pouts.

I give her another kiss, this one slightly less quick and marginally less chaste. "Good."

Then I grab my coffee mug and wander out into the backyard to find my taskmaster daughter and talk her down before her unpaid workforce of siblings and cousins revolts.

CHAPTER 27

Noelle

The day speeds by in a blur. I see Nick in passing several times, but we don't have time to talk. Even with the kinder, gentler version of Holly running the show, two o'clock is here before I know it. The Candlelight Chapel bell chimes the hour just as I put the star-shaped piece of pineapple atop the fruit Christmas tree I've created on a silver platter. Then I look down at my casual clothes.

"I need to change," I tell the closest Jolly, who turns out to be a Field.

Rosemary looks up from the vegetable Christmas tree she's arranging on an identical platter. She places a black olive with precision, then unties her apron.

"I'll walk you back to the guest house. Then we'll come back here and I'll change. Holly said the doors open at two, but people don't show up in force until closer to the happy hour."

"That's right. These first few hours will mostly be families with little ones. So Ivy and Sage will be busy with the arts and crafts, but otherwise the crowd should be light."

"Perfect. Let's go now before someone can give us another job."

I give her an apologetic smile. "I hate to ask, but all the clothes Holly pulled together for me are pretty casual. So, unless I'm going to wear the Mrs. Claus dress, I need to borrow something else. Sorry."

"Please don't apologize. It's not your fault there's a psycho out there looking for you."

Isn't it, though?

I brush the thought away and say, "You're right."

She grins. "Anyway, you're in luck. Sage always tells us that you redheads have special color concerns when it comes to your wardrobe. I have no clue if that's true, but she packed at least four dresses so she'd have options for today. Let's find her before the arts and crafts start and get you even more gorgeous."

We head into the family's living area and find Sage in the hall bathroom doing her makeup elbow to elbow with Ivy. They're wearing adorable sundresses. Sage's is, well, sage green with tiny silver polka-dots. The green definitely complements her copper-colored hair. Ivy's is red- and white-striped with fun bows on the pockets. When Rosemary announces that it's time for my makeover, they both squeal and drop their lip glosses.

Ten minutes later, I'm wearing a beautiful emerald green

sleeveless shantung silk dress that fits me like a glove. While Ivy curls my hair into wavy face-framing tendrils, Sage is giving me a smoky eye.

Merry pops her head into the bathroom. "Whoa, Dad's gonna die when he sees you. You look hot." She holds up a pair of silver sandals with a kitten heel. "I think these will fit you."

"Thanks."

She puts them down in front of me, and I step into them carefully so as to avoid a hot curling iron to the neck or a mascara wand to the eyeball. Female beauty can be a real minefield. But, let's face it, it can also be a ridiculous amount of fun—especially, when you've got good friends to get ready with. And I realize that even though all these women are twenty-some years younger than me, I consider them friends.

"The shoe fits," I announce.

"Then I guess you'll wear it," Merry says with a grin. Then she frowns at my toes. "There's a fun pearl nail polish in the other bathroom if you want to do your toes."

"Thanks. I love that jumpsuit on you."

Merry gives us a twirl and the wide, flowing legs of her deep red jumpsuit flare out. "Me, too. I learned the hard way that catering in a dress sucks peppermint balls."

"You can say *that* again," Rosemary says as she reappears, wearing a similar jumpsuit. Hers is classic black, and she's tied a red and white sash around the waist for a splash of color. She's braided her long blonde hair into an updo.

I swipe a lipstick over my mouth and we all spill out into the hallway, where we run into Holly, who's wearing a silver sheath dress and red stilettos that make my feet ache just from looking at them, and Thyme, adorable in a one-shoulder maxi dress with a diagonal stripe in muted greens and reds.

"Group picture before we start mingling!" Holly announces.

We all gather in the family room, and Holly starts messing with the timer on her camera.

"Wait. Where's your dad?" I say.

She frowns and puts down the digital camera. "I'll find him."

She rushes out of the living room and returns a moment later with Nick in tow. He does a double take. "Wow, you all look gorgeous."

"Thanks, Dad. Now squeeze in, please." Holly sets the timer and runs to stand next to Rosemary while Nick wedges himself into the picture beside me.

"You look particularly gorgeous," he whispers into my hair.

"You don't look half-bad yourself," I whisper back. It's true. He's wearing tan linen pants and a forest green linen shirt with the cuffs rolled up to his elbows.

"Smile!" Holly orders.

We smile. And smile. And smile some more while her camera clicks wildly on the mantle. When it finally stops, she grabs it and turns back to us. "Okay, let's do this."

As the Jolly and Field women disperse, Nick and I hang back. Once we're alone in the living room, he backs me up to the wall and drops a trail of kisses along my neck. I wet my lips and pull his head back to nibble on his ear.

"Mmm," I say. "Wonder what boxers you're wearing now?"

"Santa wearing a Hawaiian shirt and grilling shrimp on the barbie."

"No, you're not."

"There's only one way to find out." He raises an eyebrow.

I give him a slow smile. "Later?"

"Later." He swallows hard and backs out of the room without taking his eyes off me.

I glance down at my toes and decide Merry's right. They could use a quick coat of polish. So instead of following the others, I head back to the living quarters to grab the nail polish.

I grab it from the counter in the second bathroom and sit on the edge of the bathtub to give my toenails a coat of pearly white. Then I return the cap to the bottle, check my hair in the mirror, and go out into the hallway.

A door slams somewhere in the private wing. I frown. Nobody should be back here. I almost go to investigate the noise, but I remember my promise to Nick and what happens to characters who are TSTL and stop myself. Instead, I continue on my path back to the inn.

As I'm congratulating myself on my good judgment, I walk past the bathroom where Ivy, Sage, and I got ready, and a flash of red on the mirror catches my eye. I walk inside and stare in horror at the lipsticked letters scrawled over the glass. *Puttana.*

No, no, no. He's here. Dante is in the house.

My pulse thrums against my throat as I scrabble in the pocket of my borrowed dress for my phone to text Nick.

He's here.

My hands shake as I press send. I'm about to slip the phone back into my pocket when it's slapped out of my hand and hits the bathroom tile. I turn to see *him* lunging forward from behind the shower curtain. I open my mouth to scream, and he clamps a hand over my mouth. He drags me out of the bathroom and down the hall to the side exit.

I flail and thrash, fighting hard. Sensei Adam says, in the event of an abduction, to do whatever it takes to avoid being taken to a second location. I kick and wriggle, trying to get leverage to bite Dante's hand the way I did Nick's. But he's moving fast and I can't get a good angle.

Then he grabs a fistful of my hair and pulls me to the right, fast. An instant later, he pushes me left. My head bounces off the corner of the opposite wall and darkness creeps into the edges of my vision like someone applied a vignette filter. The darkness grows and grows, and then it's all I see as I slide to the floor.

CHAPTER 28

Nick

I'm chatting with a retired Coast Guard captain and her wife who've made the trip from Charleston, South Carolina, for Christmas in July every year for the past twelve years when my phone vibrates in my pocket. I silently curse myself for not putting it on 'do not disturb' and ignore the notification, focusing instead on Captain Tanner's story about teaching her great-nephew to sail.

When the bar opens, the Tanners excuse themselves to trade their sparkling waters for sparkling wine, and I pop into the kitchen to check on Merry and Rosemary.

"Everything good in here?"

"Easy peasy," Merry says.

"Piece of cake," Rosemary agrees.

"Speaking of cake, Holly wants me to put the snowman ice

cream cakes out at six o'clock. Mom usually waited until eight." Merry looks at me, waiting for a ruling.

I almost say eight because that's the way we've always done it, but I told Holly this was her party now. "Let's try six this year and see how it goes."

Merry shrugs. "You got it."

"Have either of you seen Noelle lately?"

I realize I haven't seen her since I had her backed up against the wall in the family room. I check my watch. That was over an hour ago.

They both shake their heads.

"No," Rosemary says.

"She's gotta be around here somewhere, though, Dad. Try not to worry," Merry says.

"I'm not worried," I promise before I head out of the kitchen.

I'm really not. Unbeknownst to Noelle, my daughters and nieces, and my guests, I spent the morning arranging a series of security measures that should make the Inn at Mistletoe Mountain impenetrable. Nobody's getting in unless I want them to. The Santa Claus Crew is set up in eight red Adirondack chairs on the front porch, and a half dozen Lords of the Mountain are scattered around the backyard playing horseshoes and badminton. Meanwhile, Griselda, Sensei Adam, and Enrique are circulating with guests. They've all been briefed on Dante Bianchi and I've passed around the mug shot Rosemary's husband emailed me. If he tries to walk into the party, he'll regret it.

I make a circuit through the parlor, the library, and the formal dining room, checking on guests and smiling at the arts and crafts project Sage and Ivy have corralled several kids into doing. I stand and watch them help our youngest guests make pipe cleaner reindeer for a few minutes before moving on.

Thyme's tending bar. She's got the toughest job, but she's wearing a big smile, moving like lightning, and cracking a steady stream of jokes, so the tip jar on the bar is already nearly full. Good for her. I'm about to go out to the porch to check in with my A Team, when Holly rushes up and grabs my arm.

"Great open house, Holly. You've done a fantastic job."

She waves off the praise as she pulls me into the hallway. "Have you seen Noelle anywhere?" she asks. Her eyebrows are knitted together, and she's chewed off most of her lipstick, which isn't like her.

My heart thumps. "No. Why?"

She screws up her face and for a second I think she's about to cry. My heart's really pounding now.

But she parts her lips and exhales slowly. Straw breathing, Griselda calls it. She taught it to Carol to help her control her anxiety when she was in hospice care, and Carol taught it to the rest of us.

"That Stillwater kid, the chess genius, does he make up stories?"

"I have no idea. Why?"

She tilts her head toward the sitting room. "Well, I hope he does because he says he saw Noelle leaving with a man."

My heart stops thrumming and drops all the way to my stomach. I run into the sitting room and skid to a stop in front of Brent Stillwater, who sits in a too-big chair, swinging his legs and sucking on an oversized candy cane.

"Hi, Mr. Jolly. Great party," he says like a little grown-up.

I remind myself he's five and crouch in front of him. "I'm glad you think so, Brent. Some of the kids are making reindeer crafts."

"No, thanks. I'm just here for the sugar."

"Fair enough." I clear my throat. "So what's this about Ms. Winters?"

He presses his lips together and shakes his head. "I think she's mad at me, but I don't know what I did that was bad. And, really, even when I *am* bad, she doesn't usually get mad."

"What makes you think she's mad now?" I ask carefully.

"She didn't say hi to me when she was leaving."

"You saw her leave?"

He nods. "I was tossing beanbags in the backyard with Sunny." He pauses. "We were also eating marshmallows."

It takes me a second to realize he's justifying playing the game because he was also eating sugar. He wouldn't want me to think he was doing a child-like activity just for fun.

"Sure, I get that. So you said hi, but she didn't answer you. Maybe she didn't hear you?" I suggest.

He considers this possibility. "Maybe. Sunny said she might have had too much to drink because the jerk guy was holding her up and helping her walk."

"What jerk guy?" I keep my tone as calm and upbeat as humanly possible even though I'm screaming inside.

"The guy who knocked over Sunny's tower yesterday," he says matter-of-factly.

I race from the room, pulling out my phone to call Deputy

Wells. And that's when I see my notification. Text from Noe. I swipe to open it and read the two-word message with horror:

He's here.

LIKE SOMETHING out of the worst Christmas song ever, eight puzzled Santas, six pissed-off bikers, three horrified nieces, two freaked-out daughters, two fitness instructors, and a retired teacher crowd around the family room looking down at Noelle's cracked phone as I recount the writing on the bathroom mirror, the blood I found in the hallway near the side exit, and the description Sunny and Brent gave me.

"How'd he get in?" Enrique says with a deep frown.

"I think must have *been* in. Maybe he checked in as a guest. I was focused on keeping people *out.* Meanwhile, the threat was inside all along." I would love to kick my own ass right now.

"Wait, where's Holly?" Ivy asks.

"She knows what's going on. But somebody has to be in charge of the party. And she's going to need some help." I stare at my daughters.

Finally, Merry raises a reluctant hand. "I should stay and take care of the food."

Rosemary, seated between her sisters, gets an elbow to each rib. "Ow! Fine, I'll help Merry. Some guy who says he's a baker also offered to help."

"Enzo?" Merry sniffs. "We don't need him."

"Great." I turn to Thyme and Sage. "The police are going to

want to interview Sunny and Brent. Brent's parents said he really took a shine to you at the library. Maybe you could sit in with him when the cops talk to him."

They nod in unison. "Sure."

Ivy narrows her eyes. "How do you plan to sideline me, Dad?"

I shake my head. "You're coming with us, actually. We need drivers because a bunch of people walked here and we don't have time to waste while they go get their cars. But you're staying in the station wagon. Are we clear?"

"We're clear," she says with an excited grin, ignoring the daggers the other members of the family are shooting at her.

Enrique raises his hand. "You think he took her back to the lodge, right?"

I hope he took her back to the lodge. Because if he left town, I don't know what to do.

"That's my current thinking."

"Why?"

"When I first told the police about the break-in, they weren't overly interested in checking it out. The deputy said even if it was Bianchi who broke in, once he saw the cardboard we taped over the window, he'd abandon it as a hideout because it wasn't safe anymore."

"Makes sense. So why are we going there?"

"Because Noelle said he's smart. And he probably realizes the police will assume he'll avoid that spot because it's not secure. So taking her there is unexpected. And he knows Brent and Sunny saw him leave with her. So he'll have to assume there's law enforcement looking for him all the way from the Canadian border to the New York airports. He'll have no choice but to lay low. The lodge is the best bet."

I must sound more confident than I feel because all around the room heads are nodding.

"Any other questions?"

Nobody says a word.

"Good. Now let's roll out before the police get here and try to stop us."

CHAPTER 29

Noelle

I come to with a banger of a headache and dust tickling my nostrils. I can't hear Dante, but I know he's in here somewhere. Wherever *here* is. I keep my eyelids mostly closed but peer out from under my eyelashes to try to get my bearings. I'm in a dark, musty, quiet room. The air is cool. I'm on my back on a couch that's covered in rough, scratchy fabric. Outside I hear birds chirping.

"Hello, Noelle."

Dante's lightly accented English is like nails on a chalkboard. I suppress a shudder and open my eyes, pulling myself up to a seated position. He's sitting in a chair on the other side of the room watching me pretend to sleep like the freak he is. We're in the old ski lodge.

"Dante."

We stare at each other for what feels like a long time. This makes me wonder how long it's been since he bashed my head against the wall and dragged me out of the inn. I glance up at the clock, but it's stopped. Stuck at ten to nine.

"What do you want?"

"I want you to stop debasing yourself with the innkeeper."

Nice.

"Still a peeping tom, I see. Well, if you know about me and Nick, then you must know I'm not available. Off the market, Dante."

In response, he spits on the floor. I take this as a possible sign of personal growth because the last time I saw Dante spit, it was aimed at my face. I have no idea why I'm sassing this unstable, violent man—other than I'm really mad. More mad than scared even. Because I am finally seizing life, living fully, and here comes a narcissistic Italian psychopath to mess it up by murdering me. This is so patently unjust that I can't even be frightened, just furious.

I try again. "But I wasn't dating Nick when you decided to flee your arrest warrant in Ravenna and come here. So why are you here?"

Anger, real anger, flashes across his face. "I read about you. Showing off your little children's library program like the *puttana* you are. Look at me, pay attention to me. So needy."

I wait a beat. Then I say, "You sound jealous, Dante."

He takes a long swig of beer from a bottle that I recognize from the open house. Then, without warning, he hurls it at me. I duck and it smashes into the wall above my head. Glass and beer rain down on me.

"Clean up the mess," he orders.

I'm about to tell him to clean up his own flipping mess, when I stop myself. Sensei Adam makes us do this brainstorming exercise where we look around the room and try to find everyday objects that we can use as weapons. A broom would make an excellent improvised weapon.

I stand up and smooth my dress over my thighs. "With what?"

He waves a hand. "There must be a broom. Find it."

I walk, unsteady as a newborn foal, across the room and toward the swinging doors that lead to the kitchen. Because a knife or even a fork would be superior to a broom. But he stops me.

"Not in there. Down the hall."

For a split second, I consider dashing into the kitchen anyway. But I'm woozy, and he's strong and evil, and I'm afraid I'll end up on the wrong end of the knife. So I turn to my left and walk until I reach a narrow closet set into the paneling.

I open it. It's crammed full of cleaning supplies. Nothing super helpful, though—like, say, lye, or bleach, or a loaded semi-automatic rifle.

"Hurry up!" he shouts.

I grab the broom and dustpan and slam the door shut. Something shiny winks up at me from the bottom of the dustpan. I squint down at it. It's a big glass shard. A wicked, sharp piece of glass. I pluck it out carefully and tuck it into my dress pocket. Now I have two weapons.

I walk back into the room and flash him a tight, unfriendly smile as I pass him to go sweep up his broken glass.

"Stop."

I stop.

"You didn't think I'd let you get your hands on that glass, did you, *puttana?*"

My heart drops. How can he possibly know? Then I realize he means the beer bottle, and I turn to face him. "So you do or do not want me to clean up the mess you made? Which is it, Dante?"

He lunges from the chair like a panther and wrenches the broom out of my hands. He throws it toward the front window. It smashes through the pane of glass next to the one someone (presumably him) already broke and sails outside, where it lands on the porch with a clatter. The clattering lasts for an unusually long time—and sounds suspiciously like feet.

Nick.

I want to cry with relief, but I need to distract Dante.

I turn back to him. "You really like to break things, huh?"

"I'd like to break you," he hisses.

I force my frozen face muscles into a slow smile. "It must really bother you that you couldn't break me all those years ago. For you to come all this way, chasing after me. Kind of pathetic."

He's going to slap me. I know he's going to slap me, and I want him to.

Sure enough, he raises his right hand and backhands me across my left cheek, whipping my head to the right.

Oof. My cheek stings. A lot. I bite my lip to keep from crying out.

He laughs. As I move my head back to face him, I slip my right hand into my pocket and wrap my fist around the piece of glass.

He's still laughing when I pull my hand out and drive the glass right into his thigh with all my might. As I'd hoped, it hits his femoral artery, which I know by the bright red blood that spurts out.

He howls and I take several quick steps back as the front door crashes open and Nick runs into the lodge, clutching a hammer. Santas and Lords stream in behind him, followed by Griselda, Sensei Adam, and Enrique.

Nick's standing over Dante, who's collapsed on the floor. I walk over and take the hammer out of his hand. "You brought the cavalry. Thank you for rescuing me."

I press a kiss to his lips.

"Looks like you rescued yourself, Noe."

He kisses me back.

I hand the hammer to Griselda and say to nobody in particular, "I stabbed him in the femoral artery. If he doesn't get first aid in the next seven minutes, he's going to bleed to death."

I swear I watch Griselda consider just letting him die. Then she sighs heavily and starts to shrug off her sparkly shawl. But one of the Lords stops her.

"I'm an emergency department doctor," he tells her with clear reluctance. "So I have a duty to save this piece of poop." He raises his voice. "I need a tourniquet!"

Well, boo. I untie the silk sash from my dress and hand it to him.

"This'll work. Thanks. Hey, how did you know where to stab him?"

"I read it in a thriller. Reading is fundamental, you know."

Nick is staring at me. "You just almost killed him *and* saved his life."

"Carol's note told me not to die regretting missed opportunities," I explain with a shrug.

"We're going to go to the hospital and get you checked out. Ivy's waiting in the car."

"Why? I'm fine."

"There's a handprint on your face, and a bloody wound on the side of your head, Noelle."

"Oh, right. Shouldn't we wait for the police, though?"

Nick turns to Santa Jamal. "You're in charge. When the police get here explain what happened and tell them they can interview Noelle at the medical center."

"You got it."

We head for the door. Nick has his arm wrapped tightly around my waist.

"Wait," I tell him when we reach the threshold.

He stops. I turn around and take in the ragtag band that rode to my rescue. My friends and neighbors.

"Thank you. All of you," I say. "I love you, and I love this town."

One of the Lords wipes away a tear. Sensei Adam makes a heart shape with his hands. Griselda snaps, "Will you get her out of here before she breaks into song?"

"Especially you, Grizzy. I love you the most," I call, as Nick drags me out to the porch.

Then, he scoops me up and carries me to the waiting station wagon.

I press my face against his neck and whisper, "I lied to Grizzy. I love you the most."

"I know, Noe. I love you, too."

CHAPTER 30

Nick
Saturday

The sun shines high in the sky as the Mapleville Merrymakers play their island Christmas original "All I Want for Christmas Is a Cider Donut." The line for Merry's frozen hot chocolate (spiked) snakes around the bandstand. Her sisters and cousins pass out free frozen hot chocolate (not spiked) to the kids waiting in line to visit Santa. This line stretches the length of the green and spills out to the street in front of the chapel, where I'm told Marley and Griselda are entertaining the back of the queue with a live dramatic reading of *A Christmas Carol*.

Beside me, Noelle smiles at the children and passes out candy canes. She's got to be the first Mrs. Claus in Mistletoe Mountain history to sport a black eye, but she pulls it off.

A little girl with a mess of dark curly hair and big eyes approaches. She clutches a note.

"Ho, ho, ho," I chortle. "Do you want to sit on Santa's lap or stand?" Usually they want to sit, but I always ask first.

She nods, and I hoist her up onto my lap. She shoves the note into my hands.

"Thank you. Hey, I know you. You're Angelica."

Another nod.

"Should I read your note now or later?"

"Later," she whispers.

I add the note to the pile to my right. "So, tell Santa what you want for Christmas in July."

The rule is no material objects. We save those for December to give the parents a break. The July requests are always creative and usually hilarious.

She looks up at me. "I want to you to bring my friend Enzo a friend."

"Enzo from the millworks?"

"Yes, he's a baker. He's really nice."

"And Enzo needs a friend, does he?"

She nods her head.

"What kind of friend?"

"A friend like you have." She points at Noelle, who gives her a smile.

"A girlfriend?"

That gets a frown. "I'm not sure if it should be a girl or a boy. Someone to love."

"Got it. Anything else?"

She shakes her head.

"Okay, get a candy cane from my friend, and enjoy the rest of the festival."

"Thanks, Santa!"

She hops down off, takes the candy cane from Noelle, and runs off in the general direction of the playground. Holly steps up and hands us each a bottle of water, then announces to the crowd that there's going to be a five-minute break for the Clauses to rehydrate.

"Just six more hours today. Then we do it all over again tomorrow. How are you holding up?" I ask Noelle.

She plants a kiss on my ear. "Aside from my aching feet, fine. I'm not sure why Mrs. Claus has to stand but you get to sit."

"Tradition."

"Hmm. This one might need an update."

"Wasn't she cute, asking for a friend for Enzo?"

"Yeah, cute." Noelle looks thoughtful. "Enzo Marino? The baker?"

"Right."

She jerks her chin toward Merry's dessert truck. "They'd be a sweet match."

I groan at the pun, then chuckle. "Already matchmaking?"

"It must be the dress," she tells me.

I eye the dress in question. "Can't wait to get you out of it, Mrs. Claus," I tell her in a low, throaty voice.

She blushes, then leans down to whisper in my ear, "And I can't wait to see which boxers you're wearing today, Santa."

"Merry Christmas in July, Noe."

"The merriest, Nick."

EPILOGUE

Noelle

Three months later

istletoe Mountain's Holly, Jolly Diwali Festival is in full swing. The name may be a groaner, but the festival itself is lit. Literally and figuratively. This year the Festival of Lights coincides with Halloween, so the town is illuminated with string lights, lanterns, candle-lit jack-o'-lanterns, as well as glowing bats, witches, and ghosts that decorate windows and doors. Children zig-zag across the lawn, laughing and chasing each other, their glow-in-the-dark neon bracelets blurry streaks as they run by.

I let out a contented sigh and snuggle into Nick's side. He nuzzles my neck. The porch swing he installed on his—*our*—back porch sways as we sit and watch the festivities. I have boxes still waiting to be unpacked in the house, but they'll just have to wait. I'm taking Dickens and Carol at their word. Every day, I find at least one opportunity to grab with both hands. It's funny how easy they are to find when you're looking for them.

Like, for instance, saying yes when Nick asked me to move in. Ivy's moved out and convinced Merry to give up her apartment. They're living in my cottage, not because we don't want Ivy here, but because she got tired of walking in on us making out. I can't help it. I can't keep my hands off her father.

His neck nuzzling turns into nibbling, and I giggle, pulled out of my reverie.

"Are you okay?" he asks.

I know he's asking about my deposition. I nod. He must've offered to come with me a thousand times, but I had Holly and Marley, and, honestly, I think he was offering in part to get a break from his sister. MJ and Bart came up for a weekend visit. They would've stayed longer, but their parole officer wasn't amused and made them return to New Jersey, pronto. I have a sneaking suspicion *he* might have tipped off the Fields' PO.

"Hello?" he prompts.

"Right. The deposition. It was fine, honestly. It was a video thing, and I didn't have to see Dante's disgusting face." And it means I won't have to go to Italy for the trial, either.

Dante Bianchi was extradited to Italy because the person he kidnapped there was a *judge's* daughter. So he's definitely getting the book—or, in this case, *il libro*—thrown at him. And as the result of some legal mumbo-jumbo that Holly and Marley told me I didn't need to understand, the crimes he committed here will be taken into account when he's sentenced. *And* the judge is reexamining the police complaint I filed in Ravenna back when dinosaurs roamed the earth as part of Dante's psychological assessment. Long story short, he's going to be in prison for a long, long time. Probably the rest of his life.

"Really fine?" He cups my face in his hands and studies me.

"Better than fine," I promise.

He drops a kiss on my nose. "Good."

Delphina and Holly cruise by with sparklers in hand to pass out to the kids before the fireworks start. Holly seems to be weathering the aftermath of finding her dickweasel fiancé shagging his (and her) boss in a closet. But I'm keeping an eye on her, just in case.

"You know," Nick muses, "it's fitting that you testified today."

"Why's that?"

"Because Diwali celebrates the triumph of light over darkness, good over evil, hot librarians over Italian creeps."

"I think you made up that last part, but your erudition is sexy."

In response, he smothers me with kisses.

Of course, Griselda picks this precise moment to walk by and shake her head. "Don't you two *have* a room?"

"We don't want to miss the fireworks," Nick tells her. I wait for it. "But don't worry, Grizzy, we'll be making our own fireworks later, if you know what I mean."

"Everyone knows what you mean, Nick." She rolls her eyes, but she's smiling when she walks away.

"Speaking of the fireworks, it's almost time."

He nods, then he says, "We forgot to do three things at dinner." His voice is strangled and weirdly high-pitched.

"I guess we did. What's wrong with your voice?"

"Nothing," he squeaks. Then he coughs and pitches his voice lower, "Nothing."

"If you say so."

"Let's do it now while we wait for the fireworks. What's one thing you're grateful for?"

"That I got back to town in time to see the parade. You?"

"That I woke up to your beautiful face sleeping next to me and that I get to do it every day."

Wow, okay. His is better than mine. I need to take it up a notch.

"One thing you regret?" he asks.

I think for a minute. "I regret that I tried to discourage you from joining the Lords of the Mountain. You're sexy on your motorcycle, and I get a friends of the club discount from my ophthalmologist now. Win, win. You?"

"No regrets today."

I narrow my eyes. "I thought you said that's not allowed?"

He huffs. "Fine, I suppose I regret reporting my sister and her husband to their parole officer."

"I knew it!" I poke him in the ribs, and he catches my hand between his.

"What are you going to do to make tomorrow a brighter day?"

I whisper in his ear. "I've been taking private lessons with Griselda. I've got something to show you involving that pole you had installed in the bedroom."

"That sounds like a thing you're going to do tonight."

"And tomorrow. And the next day and the day after that," I tell him. Assuming I don't fall on my face the first time. But

Grizzy says my gyrations are almost acceptable now, so I'm hopeful.

I look at him expectantly, waiting for him to tell me what he's going to do. But he's staring at his watch.

"Nick?"

"Just checking. Less than a minute until the fireworks start."

As he says the words, the sky lights up with pinks, golds, and purples. I keep my eyes on the pyrotechnics display over the trees and say, "What are you going to do to make tomorrow a better day?"

Another firework explodes. This one's my favorite kind—a white spray that reminds me of a weeping willow tree.

Nick still has my hand trapped when he says, "This is what I'm going to do."

I drag my eyes away from the sky in time to see him slip a dazzling emerald onto my ring finger.

My heart thumps so loudly it could be a firework.

"Noe, will you make every day for the rest of my life better and brighter by marrying me?"

I launch myself into his lap and kiss him greedily. "Yes, of course. Yes."

He pulls me against his chest and, together, we watch the fireworks celebrate light over darkness, good over evil, love over hate.

Thank you for reading *Home for Christmas in July!* Ready for more of the Jollys? You can find *Booked for Christmas,* the next book in this series wherever books are sold.

Want more of the Field sisters? Rosemary, Sage, and Thyme have their own rom-com mystery series, find them on my website www.melissafmiller.com.

All my books. If you're new to my books, you have a lot of choices! The website contains an up-to-date list of *all* my books.

A NOTE FROM MELISSA

This seed for this book was planted in the Autumn/Winter of 2020. I love—*love*—the holidays, but for obvious reasons, that year, I wasn't feeling festive. To be honest, I was really sad.

One night, I flipped on a Hallmark Christmas movie to see what all the fuss was about. And, boom, I was hooked! I'm not really a big television watcher, but that year, Christmas movies played every night at my house as I vicariously experienced all the Christmas festivities and family gatherings that were canceled in real-life through the soft-focused, small-town shenanigans of big city career women home for the holidays.

My teenagers mocked me relentlessly until my beloved husband told them to just "let Mom have this small joy." And so I watched and watched. And then, I watched some more. Those movies were a lifeline.

This pattern repeated in the winters of 2021 through 2023. I didn't watch *quite* as many as I did that first year, and I quickly realized certain storylines (mysteries) appealed to me more than others. But I kept coming back for a reliable dose of happiness. Then, I started mixing holiday women's fiction, holiday romances, and holiday mysteries in with my steady diet of crime fiction books.

And now, here we are, in Mistletoe Mountain. In a very real sense, I wrote *Home for Christmas in July* for me. But I also wrote it for you, to remind you of the light.

Longtime readers will not be surprised to learn that Mistletoe Mountain is intended to be a series. I seem to be constitutionally incapable of writing standalone books.

But why is the first book set in July, and not December? Because, dear reader, the residents of Mistletoe Mountain know that humans need love, connection, and joy all through the year.

Merrily,
Melissa

ABOUT THE AUTHOR

USA Today bestselling author Melissa F. Miller majored in English literature with concentrations in creative writing poetry and medieval literature and was stunned, upon graduation, to learn that there's not a robust job market for such a degree. After working as an editor for several years, she returned to school to earn a law degree.

After practicing law for fifteen years, including a stint as a clerk for a federal judge, nearly a decade as an attorney at major international law firms, and several years running a two-person law firm with her lawyer-husband, she turned in her bar card to make up stories instead.

Now, powered by coffee, she writes full-time from the Pennsylvania home she shares with her family and their cat and dog. (The cat's in charge.)